— THE —

New, Improved

GRETCHEN HUBBARD

ILENE COOPER

Other books in
The Kids from Kennedy Middle School series

The Kids From
KENNEDY MIDDLE SCHOOL
— THE —
New, Improved
GRETCHEN
HUBBARD
ILENE COOPER

MORROW JUNIOR BOOKS
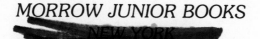
NEW YORK

For Meredith,
none better

1 2 3 4 5 6 7 8 9 10

Library of Congress Cataloging-in-Publication Data
Cooper, Ilene.
The new, improved Gretchen Hubbard / Ilene Cooper.
p.   cm.—(The Kids from Kennedy Middle School)
Summary: Formerly "Hippo Hubbard" of the sixth grade, Gretchen
slims down but feels uncomfortable receiving compliments
and attention from her classmates.
ISBN 0-688-08432-X (trade)
[1. Weight control—Fiction.   2. Self-perception—Fiction.
3. Schools—Fiction.]   I. Title.   II. Series: Cooper, Ilene.
The Kids from Kennedy Middle School
PZ7.C7856Ne 1992 [Fic]—dc20   92-6197   CIP   AC

C H A P T E R
ONE

Robin Miller frowned. "I don't think I can look at another pair of turquoise earrings."

Thank heavens, Gretchen Hubbard thought to herself.

Then something in the display case caught Robin's eye. "But maybe I can look at one more ring," Robin said as she gestured toward a weary-looking salesgirl to come and help her.

The girls, who lived in Forest Glen, Illinois, had been in Santa Fe for three days, visiting Gretchen's mother, who taught writing at a local college. They had done a lot of sightseeing, visiting small adobe churches and museums, but there were plenty of stores in Santa Fe, too, and it seemed to Gretchen as if she and Robin had been inside every one of them.

"You know, I never really liked to shop," Robin commented as the salesgirl got out the tray of rings.

"You could have fooled me," Gretchen replied with a laugh.

Gretchen didn't like to shop very much either, especially for clothes. What was the point of even looking at clothes when you were too fat to fit into them?

However, for the past couple of months she had been on a diet, and to her surprise, the pounds had actually begun falling away. She had tried dieting a couple of times before but had wound up weighing more than when she'd begun. This time, though, Gretchen had been determined. She was tired of having girls like Veronica Volner, the acknowledged queen of the sixth grade, make fun of her. Now, whenever she wanted a slice of cake or an ice-cream cone, Gretchen conjured up Veronica's smirking face. It had turned out to be a great motivator.

Her dad had promised Gretchen that when she lost ten pounds, she could buy some new clothes. Ten, twelve, fifteen pounds had disappeared, but the only purchase Gretchen had made lately was a couple of pairs of socks she needed for the trip. She was afraid that buying new clothes would be a jinx. She was sure that somehow, once those new, smaller-size jeans and tops made themselves comfortable in her closet, the weight would come back with a vengeance. It would probably happen all at once, while she was asleep.

"What do you think of this one?" Robin held out her hand. The silver ring with the greenish blue stone distracted Gretchen from the picture in her mind: a formerly thin Gretchen getting up one morning to find she was bursting out of her pajamas.

"It's nice." It didn't really look that different from the other rings Robin had tried on.

Robin stared hard at the ring. "Better than that one we saw in the shop across the street?"

Gretchen started to giggle, and Robin had to laugh, too. "I know, which ring? Which shop?"

"You have tried on a lot of jewelry," Gretchen agreed.

"My parents gave me forty dollars to spend on something nice, and I want to get the right thing." She peered down at her hand. "This isn't it."

As they walked out into the bright spring sunshine, Robin said, "Boy, I can't imagine a place more different from Forest Glen."

Forest Glen was a cozy little suburb of Chicago on the shores of Lake Michigan. It had green trees and people who looked pretty much alike. The highest thing in view were the McDonald's golden arches at the edge of town.

In Santa Fe, there were mountains in the distance and different kinds of people. "I agree," Gretchen said, looking around the town square, where several Native Americans were selling their intricately designed jewelry. "I've never noticed any Indians in *our* downtown."

"I haven't really done much looking outside the shops." Robin glanced pleadingly at Gretchen. "Do you mind if I . . . ?"

"Go ahead," Gretchen said. "I'll meet you over by that store on the corner, where they sell fudge."

Robin stared at Gretchen.

"I didn't say I was going to have any," Gretchen replied, unruffled. "It's just an easy place to meet."

Not that she would have minded some fudge. Her stomach lurched a little at the thought. Just because she had been successful at dieting didn't mean that visions of fudge and cookies had stopped dancing around in her head. Here, far from Veronica and the other girls who had made fun of her, Gretchen could almost believe that she didn't have to be quite so vigilant about her weight. She idly wondered if the shop made Rocky Road.

Stop it, Gretchen said silently. You've had hundreds of pieces of fudge in your life. They all taste the same.

With determination, she walked into one of the women's boutiques. Even looking at clothes was better than thinking about food.

Like many of the other stores in Santa Fe, this one was decorated Western-style. Dresses and blouses hung on timber racks, and Navaho blankets were draped over chairs. There were a number of clothes shops in Forest Glen, but it was doubtful you could buy a cowboy hat at any of them.

Gretchen moved to make way for a smiling couple and unexpectedly caught sight of herself in a full-length mirror. She was taken aback. Could this thin blond girl looking at her actually be the person known as Hippo Hubbard?

A saleswoman came up behind her. "Would you like to see something?"

Gretchen guiltily turned away from the mirror. "No, no. Just looking." Then she got more embarrassed because it sounded as if "just looking" at herself was a reasonable way to while away the minutes. Since Gretchen had spent most of the last four or five years avoiding mirrors, the irony of seeming so conceited was not lost on her.

Without a further glance at the denim shirts or shirtwaist dresses, Gretchen hurried out of the store. Now, for some reason, she really did feel like having a piece of fudge. Before she could give in to the temptation, Robin came hurrying up to her.

"Gretchen, come with me. I want to show you something."

Robin's good-natured face was so full of enthusiasm, Gretchen had to smile. She had spent so many years without real friends that it still seemed like a small miracle that she and Robin were close again, the way they had been in the first and second grades. Veronica Volner had come between them, but her meanness had finally driven Robin away.

When Mrs. Hubbard left Forest Glen last fall to take this teaching job, she had planned for Gretchen to visit her over spring break. At the time, Gretchen had assumed she'd be going alone, but as her friendship with Robin blossomed, Gretchen had toyed with the idea of asking her mother if Robin could come, too. She tentatively broached the subject, and Mrs. Hubbard had been delighted that Gretchen was close enough with Robin to want her along. The Millers had given their consent, and Gretchen and Robin were feverish with excitement until the day of departure finally arrived. Robin had told Gretchen more than once what a great time she was having, and Gretchen was pleased that she could repay Robin in some small way for all the nice things she had done for her in the past couple of months.

Robin led Gretchen toward a woman with long black braids who was standing behind a tray of rings and earrings. Robin looked at her inquiringly, and when the woman nodded, Robin slipped on a silver ring with a black stone raised in the middle.

"It's not turquoise," Gretchen said with surprise.

"Onyx," the woman informed her.

"I was getting tired of turquoise," Robin said.

"Me, too," Gretchen agreed fervently. She examined the ring on Robin's outstretched hand. "I like it. It's different."

"This lady made it," Robin said.

"You did?" Despite all the jewelry she had looked at in the past few days, Gretchen had never really thought about the fact that someone actually fashioned the pieces.

The woman tossed one of her braids over her shoulder. "My name is engraved in the band."

Robin took off the ring and squinted at the inside. "J. Birdsong. Pretty name," she said.

"I think you should get it," Gretchen said stoutly.

"It's forty-five dollars."

"I could lend you the rest."

"How much do you have?" the woman asked.

"Forty dollars for my special present, but I could come up with five more."

"Don't bother. It's yours," the woman said, smiling for the first time.

Robin dug around in her purse until she came up with the wad of money she had hidden at the bottom of the bag. She counted out forty dollars and handed the money to J. Birdsong.

"What do you want to do now?" Gretchen asked as they walked away.

"Let's go back to the apartment and go swimming."

Mrs. Hubbard's apartment complex had a deliciously cool-looking outdoor pool, and Robin had been wanting to go swimming in it ever since they arrived. From force of habit, Gretchen had avoided swimming. Lounging around the pool was not Hippo Hubbard's favorite activity, but after seeing herself looking so svelte in the dress shop, Gretchen decided she might as well put on her bathing suit and dive in—literally.

Mrs. Hubbard's apartment was within walking distance of the square, as long as you didn't mind a long walk. By the time the girls arrived, Gretchen was perspiring so badly that she was actually looking forward to the swim.

"What time is your mother coming home?" Robin asked as they entered the blessedly cool apartment.

"She'll be home for dinner. She said we might go out to a restaurant in the mall."

"Southwestern food?" Robin asked as she walked into the guest room that she and Gretchen were sharing.

Gretchen knew that Robin was getting a little weary of all the tortillas, beans, and spices that went along with the local food. "Pizza," she responded.

"All right!" Robin flopped down on the bed.

Glancing at her watch, Gretchen said, "If you really want to go to the pool, we should get a move on."

"Okay," Robin said agreeably. She got up and began rummaging through a drawer for her bathing suit.

Gretchen knew right where her suit was. She hadn't unpacked it yet. By the time she opened her case and dug it out, Robin was already preening in front of the mirror in her pink polka-dot two-piece. "Do you think I look fat?" she asked, turning around. Realizing what she had said, Robin's cheeks grew as red as her hair.

"It's okay," Gretchen said quietly. "I'm not fat anymore."

"You're sure not."

"Of course, you never were."

"I know. But sometimes I worry that I am." Robin looked down at herself. "Especially in a bathing suit."

"Well, I guess I should change now." Gretchen wished she could go into the bathroom to change, but Robin had put on her suit in the bedroom, and Gretchen didn't want Robin to think she was weird. Of course, she had more reason to be shy than Robin. The rest of her might be getting smaller, but her chest seemed to be getting bigger every day.

Mrs. Hubbard had mentioned it when she and Gretchen had settled down on the couch for a talk that first night, after Robin had fallen asleep. "You're really growing up," her mother said, lightly touching Gretchen's hair.

"I *am* getting taller."

"That, too," Mrs. Hubbard said with a slight smile.

"Oh, I know what you mean." Gretchen looked at the wall.

"It's nothing to be ashamed of, Gretchen. I'm glad when I was home at Christmas we got you those bras."

Gretchen was too embarrassed to tell her mother they already seemed to be tight. Now, with Robin just standing there, waiting for her to change, Gretchen could feel herself flushing again.

"Hey, I forgot to bring a beach robe," Robin said.

"There's a terry-cloth robe hanging on my mother's bathroom door. I'm sure she wouldn't mind if you wore that one."

"Really?"

"Of course not."

The second Robin was out the door, Gretchen wiggled out of her clothes and slipped on her faded old suit. She was just pulling it up when Robin came back. As Robin caught sight of Gretchen, she frowned.

"What's wrong?" Gretchen asked. "I know it's old . . ."

"It's way too big."

"It is?" Gretchen walked over to the full-length mirror. The shapeless suit hung on her, except around the top. Gretchen stood there uncertainly. "Maybe I should just put on some shorts and sit by the pool. This does look pretty dopey."

"Why don't we buy you a new suit?"

Gretchen turned to see her mother standing in the doorway. "You're home early."

"I don't want to miss a minute with you two."

"We were going to swim until it was time to eat."

Mrs. Hubbard nodded cheerily. "Let's all go. I think I have a suit that will fit you, Gretchen. Then when we're at the mall, we can look for something new and pretty." She pointed to the suit Gretchen was wearing. "That we can use for rags."

Gretchen had never thought of her mother as interested in clothes. Mrs. Hubbard usually ran around in jeans and a T-shirt, or a flannel shirt if the weather was cold. But her indifference to fashion didn't seem to apply when it came to Gretchen. She chattered all through dinner about what they should get.

"You're thin enough for leggings." She turned to Robin. "It's mostly that or jeans, right?"

Robin tried to answer through her pizza. "Yes."

Mrs. Hubbard frowned. "But those big tops the kids wear aren't going to show off your new figure."

Fine, Gretchen thought. She didn't want to show off her new figure anyway. She liked being thinner, but she didn't want to call attention to herself. That's why she hadn't bought any new clothes back home.

"Blue," her mother continued. "With your beautiful blue eyes, we ought to stick with blues."

Gretchen put down her bite of salad. "Mom, I don't really need that much."

"Yes, you do."

Gretchen could feel herself getting angry. She glanced at Robin, who just shrugged and said, "Shopping's fun."

Maybe for some people. It had always been one of the most miserable experiences of her life. She could remember when she was very young, six or seven, taking the train into Chicago with her mother to a store that had actually had the horrid name of The Chubby Shop. The only good thing about The Chubby Shop was that it was so far away no one knew that she had to buy her clothes there. The bad things started as soon as you walked through the door. You were greeted by a saleslady who obviously knew something about being chubby. She was as wide as she was tall.

For some reason whoever bought the merchandise for the store believed that chubby girls looked best in flowered dresses with puffed sleeves and sashes that cut the body in half—like a bedspread tied in the middle. Trying on those ugly dresses, one after another, was agony. The saleslady made it worse by saying that Gretchen looked "charming" or "adorable." Even at seven, Gretchen knew that "horrible" would have been a better adjective.

She had made more of a fuss about going to The Chubby Shop than she did about visiting the dentist, and eventually her mother had just given in and allowed Gretchen to buy bigger sizes that had to be altered for length at regular department stores. She wore a lot of pants with elastic at the waist and big, sloppy sweaters or blouses, hoping that no one would notice what was underneath. Everyone did anyway. Veronica took every opportunity to remind Gretchen that she had more jiggle to the wiggle than anyone she had ever seen.

Now, however, as they browsed the stores, shopping did seem almost fun. When her mother suggested a pair of black and white polka-dot shorts, Gretchen had gone immediately to the end of the rack, where the larger sizes were, but she could tell at a glance they would be too big. It was a pleasure to try on the shorts in the same size anyone else would wear. They looked cute, too. By the end of the evening, she had gotten the shorts, a coordinating black blouse, the promised bathing suit, a blue cotton sweater, some leggings, a Santa Fe T-shirt, and a sleeveless dress that was miles away from the kind she used to buy at The Chubby Shop. There was so much stuff, it took the three of them to carry the bags.

"Quite a haul," her mother commented as they rode down the escalator.

"Did I get too much?" Gretchen asked in a worried voice.

"Of course not," Mrs. Hubbard declared. "We have to make up for a couple of years." Glancing down the escalator, she said, "They're having a linen sale here and I need some sheets. Do you want to stay with me or meet me on the first floor?"

Makeup, jewelry, and hair accessories were downstairs. "The first floor," the girls said in unison.

They stopped first to look at the earrings. Robin had recently had her ears pierced. "I love my ring, but I wish I had a few more dollars to spend," she said, fingering a pair of dangly silver hearts.

After Robin had tried on a pink comb in her curly red hair and Gretchen had examined a polka-dot headband, the girls came to the makeup counter. A young woman, wearing a white smock and looking a trifle bored, glanced at Gretchen. "Would you like to have a make-over?"

Gretchen looked startled. "I don't think so. I mean I don't usually wear makeup." Usually? she thought to herself. Never.

Robin nudged her. "Oh, go ahead."

The woman smiled slightly. "The whole purpose of these make-overs is to get the customer to buy the cosmetics. But, hey, it's almost closing time, and putting a little lipstick and eye shadow on you would be more fun than just watching the big hand get closer to the twelve."

Gretchen shrugged, trying to look nonchalant. "In that case . . ."

By the time her mother found them, about ten minutes later, Gretchen had learned the proper way to outline her lips, dab on eye shadow, and wear mascara.

"Your blond hair with your blue eyes is just a classic combination," the cosmetician was commenting. "And your skin's so nice you don't need any cheek color."

"I should say she doesn't." Mrs. Hubbard was frowning.

"It's just for fun, Mom," Gretchen said, sliding off the high stool.

"I hope you don't mind," the salesgirl cut in smoothly. "She can take it all off with cold cream when she gets home. I know she's a little young for makeup, but the lip gloss would be appropriate. And perhaps the eye shadow?"

Mrs. Hubbard just shook her head. "You look fifteen."

"Don't worry," Gretchen said nervously, "I'll get it all off."

"Would you be interested in the lip gloss?" the salesgirl asked.

"No, she wouldn't," her mother answered. Then Mrs. Hubbard softened. "As long as you know you're not allowed to wear makeup yet, Gretchen, I guess it was all right to experiment this once."

Gretchen noticed Robin staring at her. "Gretchen, you're beautiful."

"Yeah, right." Gretchen laughed.

Robin picked up the hand mirror from the counter. "Take a look."

Gretchen took the mirror. She didn't know what she was expecting, but certainly not this.

Looking back at her was a girl with high cheekbones, a lush pink mouth, and sparkling eyes. Gretchen licked her lips, and so did the girl.

She had always wanted to be pretty. Now it seemed she was.

C H A P T E R
TWO

"Why are you walking all hunched over like that?" Robin asked as she and Gretchen approached Kennedy Middle School.

"Was I?" Gretchen responded, but she knew it was true. She felt self-conscious.

"You look great!"

Gretchen supposed she did. At least better than she could ever remember. She was wearing the new leggings and blue sweater she had gotten in Santa Fe. Tentatively, she touched her hair. She still couldn't get used to its being short.

It was all her mother's fault. Mrs. Hubbard had suggested a haircut the night of her makeover. Robin had said good night and fallen into bed as soon as they got home, but Gretchen and her mother hadn't been sleepy.

"I didn't like your wearing all that makeup, hon, but you sure did look pretty."

"I did?"

"Of course you did. You know that."

"I guess I looked okay," Gretchen replied shyly.

Mrs. Hubbard fingered a string of Gretchen's blond hair. "Maybe you should get your hair cut."

"Do you think so?" Gretchen asked, startled.

"Now that your face is so thin, I think a short haircut would look adorable."

Gretchen felt tears welling up in her eyes. Not because her mother thought she should cut her hair, but because she realized how much she was going to miss her mom once she was back home.

Mrs. Hubbard seemed to sense her thoughts. "I know these last few months haven't been easy for you, Gretchen. I guess they haven't been easy for any of us."

Suddenly Gretchen's sad feelings became mixed with anger. As far as she could tell, her mother was having a fine old time in Santa Fe. Gretchen was the one who had been stuck at home, putting up with Veronica, struggling with her weight, worrying about whether this separation between her parents was permanent. She drew away from her mother.

"You're mad at me?"

Gretchen tried to pretend she wasn't. "No."

Mrs. Hubbard sighed. "I suppose you have a right. I really can't expect you to understand why I wanted to take this job so much."

"I know, I know." Gretchen chanted the reasons. "It's hard to get a job teaching writing, and your friend was head of the department here. You'd have time to do your own writing. . . ."

"And your father and I needed some time apart," Mrs. Hubbard added.

"But you and I didn't," Gretchen said, finally letting her bitterness show.

Gretchen thought she might cry, but instead, it was her mother's eyes that filled with tears. "No, that's true."

"Mom . . ."

"It's okay." Mrs. Hubbard snuffled a little into a handkerchief she pulled from her pocket. Then she tried to smile at Gretchen. "I know you've been wondering what's going to happen next."

"You said you were only going to be in New Mexico for the school year," Gretchen replied carefully.

"I know. Honey, it's not like I haven't missed you and your dad, too. I thought taking this job and being able to do my own writing away from everything would be the answer. I have loved the writing part," she added fiercely. "At home I was trying to take care of you and Dad *and* work at the bank, even though I loathed it. I was so frustrated. I hated banking, but even after finishing my master's degree I couldn't get a job writing. There never seemed to be enough time to do what I wanted." She sighed again. "But I've spent the whole year just wanting to be in two places at once."

So come home, Gretchen wanted to say, but she didn't.

"You know the school has asked me to come back next fall."

"But you're not. . . ."

"I've got a few more weeks before I need to make a decision, and I'm going to spend that time thinking about what's best for all of us."

I know what's best for me, Gretchen thought.

"For now, can't we just enjoy the rest of your vacation?" Mrs. Hubbard asked.

Gretchen nodded. She locked up the hurt feelings she felt about her parents' separation.

She had always been pretty good at pretending things didn't hurt her.

Mrs. Hubbard seemed relieved. "Good. Let's keep our minds on all the fun things we haven't done yet. I want to take you to Taos and to see a pueblo." She ruffled Gretchen's hair. "And I want to get you a really terrific haircut."

Gretchen shrugged. She didn't care much about her hair one way or the other. But the next morning, she and Robin and her mother went to a sleek hair salon, all chrome and mirrors. "We want a wonderful haircut for my daughter," Mrs. Hubbard told the stylist, pushing Gretchen forward.

Gretchen eyed the young woman apprehensively. Her wild dark hair was streaked with strands of red. "Just a regular haircut," Gretchen said.

The woman smiled. "Conservative, right?"

"Not too conservative," Robin piped up. Gretchen shot her a "keep quiet" look.

"I think you'd look great with something short and easy to take care of," the stylist said, running her hand through Gretchen's hair.

Gretchen felt like an innocent sheep about to get sheared for the first time. The sheep had no say in what was about to happen, and Gretchen didn't feel as if she did either.

Each snip of the scissors was nerve-racking, but when the stylist handed her the mirror to get an overall look, Gretchen had been amazed. The cut was almost boyish, but with gel spiking it up a little, it really looked great.

At least she had felt that way in Santa Fe. Now, walking toward school, she just felt stupid. Back here, she was still Hippo Hubbard. She had a feeling Veronica Volner would have plenty to say about a hippo trying to turn into a swan.

She was keeping an eye out for Veronica when she saw Sharon hurrying toward them. Sharon was her closest friend next to Robin.

Sharon stopped short. "Gretchen!" she squealed. "What happened to you?"

Gretchen cringed.

"Doesn't she look great?" Robin said enthusiastically.

"You look like a different person," Sharon replied wonderingly.

"Well, I guess that's good," Gretchen muttered.

Sharon fell in beside them. "Boy, you'd be the number-one topic of conversation if it wasn't for Bobby Glickman."

"Bobby?" Robin asked. "What about him?"

"He's in a movie."

"A movie?" Gretchen was startled. "He's in Hollywood?"

"No. They're shooting it around here."

This was big news. "Tell us," Robin demanded.

"I don't really know the details. I just heard that this movie about a bunch of boys is being made in Chicago and up here in the suburbs. Bobby got a part. I suppose because he's been in some television commercials."

"Boy," Robin said, "some people have all the luck. I was in a television spot, too, and no one wanted me for a movie." Robin and Sharon took drama lessons at Beech Street Theater, a local company. Earlier in the year, Robin had been picked to be in a public-service message about drugs. "Is Bobby one of the stars?" Robin asked.

"I don't think so."

"I'll ask Jonathan. He'll know." Robin and Jonathan liked each other, and Bobby was one of Jon's best friends. Robin's cheeks reddened a little. "There he is now."

Tall, lanky Jonathan Rossi stood talking on the front steps with another of his friends, Ham Berger. Ham's real first name was Kevin, but Ham was such a natural for him. He was round, freckled, and so lazy that if he really were a hamburger, no doubt he'd enjoy lying in a pan while someone flipped him around.

"Have you talked to Jonathan since we got back?" Gretchen whispered.

Robin shook her head. "He was at his aunt's until last night."

Touching her hair, Gretchen followed Robin and Sharon over to where the boys were huddled. Gretchen knew that Jonathan would be too polite to say anything about her new look. Ham, however, was a different story.

Jonathan seemed as nervous as Robin as they exchanged hellos. He barely glanced at Gretchen and Sharon. However, Ham looked at Gretchen, and then he looked again. "Hubbard, what happened to you?"

"Nothing," she replied stiffly.

Ham punched Jonathan, who turned his attention to Gretchen. "Hey, you look good," Jon said approvingly.

"Doesn't she?" Robin said happily.

"Did you two have fun in Santa Fe?"

Robin nodded.

"You must have gone to one of those fat farms, right?" Ham asked. "Where they give you a lettuce leaf with some ketchup and call it dinner. My mom's always talking about those places." He looked at Gretchen critically. "And they scalped you there, too, right?"

"Oh, Ham," Sharon groaned. "Gretchen's haircut is totally awesome."

"I didn't say it wasn't awesome," Ham said indignantly. "I just said it was kind of short."

Gretchen wondered if there were any stores open this early. Stores that sold hats.

"Don't pay any attention to him," Robin counseled. "Look at *his* hair."

Gretchen had to smile. Ham had gotten a buzz cut during spring break.

"Why he's practically bald," Sharon sniffed.

Ham ran his hand over his head. "It's what all the sports guys wear," he said in a hurt voice.

"Oh, and what's your sport, Ham? Pie-eating competitions?" Veronica Volner laughed as she came up behind Ham.

"Get lost," Ham muttered so quietly even Veronica didn't hear him.

Veronica's eyes shifted over to Gretchen. My turn, Gretchen thought with despair. But all Veronica said was, "So you're not the only one with short hair, Ham."

Gretchen braced herself for more, but Veronica turned to Robin and asked, "What's all this about Bobby being in a movie?"

27

Robin shrugged. "I was just going to ask Jon."

"It happened right before I left for my aunt's," Jon responded as all eyes turned in his direction. "There was this casting call for a movie that's called *The Pick Pockets* or something like that. Bobby's agent sent him down, and he got a part. It's just a small one, I think."

"A small part in a movie. I wouldn't mind that," Sharon said dreamily.

"He should introduce us to the stars," Veronica piped up. "Who are the stars anyway?"

No one seemed to know.

"Well, I guess I'll have to find out." Veronica sighed, making it clear that only she could be trusted to realize what was important and accomplish it.

The first bell rang, and Veronica hurried away. The rest of the kids drifted toward the redbrick building, none of them very eager to get back to class after vacation.

Gretchen held back a little, waiting to see if Robin wanted to walk with Jonathan. She needn't have bothered. Ham was dragging Jon toward school, talking excitedly and waving his free arm. Jonathan looked back at Robin with an apologetic expression.

"I don't think I've ever seen Ham move that fast," Sharon commented.

"Yeah, and it still wasn't all that fast," Robin replied.

"But Veronica sure was speedy," Sharon said. "Off to get the scoop on Bobby."

"Did you notice she wasn't mean to you?" Robin asked Gretchen.

"I couldn't help but notice. Normally, she would have said something like, 'I didn't know they had beauty shops for balloon butts.'" Gretchen winced as she uttered the remark.

"She can't call you names like that anymore," Sharon said. "You're not fat."

Gretchen stared at Sharon, who seemed totally unaware that she had said anything special. Well, it might not mean much to Sharon, but "You're not fat" was a phrase that hadn't been used much in conjunction with her. She couldn't believe that Sharon had said it so nonchalantly.

"Told you," Robin whispered.

Gretchen gave her a grateful smile, but her expression quickly became puzzled. "That still doesn't explain why Veronica was so . . . *nice* isn't the right word. Not horrible? She could have made fun of my haircut even without my being fat."

"You know," Robin said thoughtfully,

29

"before we left, I ran into Veronica, and she said a weird thing. We were in the drugstore, standing in line and kind of pretending like we didn't see each other, when all of a sudden, she blurted out, 'I'm thinking of changing.'"

"What did she mean?"

"I didn't have a clue. As far as I knew, she meant changing from one fancy outfit into another. I didn't answer her, and she just shut up and paid for her stuff. But maybe she meant changing her personality or something."

Sharon snorted. "I don't think that a change would do it," she said as the friends entered Kennedy. "Maybe a personality transplant."

After the girls put away their books, they hurried into their classroom. Mrs. Volini, nicknamed Mt. Volini because she so easily blew her stack, hated her students to be late. The room was filling up with kids eager to exchange news and gossip about their vacations.

Gretchen immediately felt shy again. She tried to slide into her seat unnoticed, but a few eyes had already turned in her direction. Fortunately, Mrs. Volini began rapping on her desk with a ruler for attention.

"Welcome back for the last part of your sixth-grade year. We have a lot to accomplish before the end of school."

The class groaned, causing Mrs. Volini to rap even harder. "That was not the response I was looking for! I have all sorts of interesting projects planned for us."

Who was this "us"? Gretchen wondered.

"We will be studying the Bill of Rights," Mrs. Volini said, "with special emphasis on freedom of the press. In conjunction with that, I think it would be fun to start a class newspaper."

Now that did sound interesting, Gretchen thought. From the buzz around the room, the rest of the kids apparently agreed.

"But before we get down to work," Mrs. Volini continued, "I'd like to hear what some of you did over vacation. Anyone do anything exciting?" She looked around and did a double take when she saw Gretchen.

Oh, no, Gretchen prayed, please don't let her call on me.

Before Mrs. Volini could invite Gretchen up to the front, Ham Berger began waving his hand wildly. "Mrs. Volini, ask Bobby."

Mrs. Volini frowned. "We don't volunteer other students, Kevin. Why don't you come up and tell us about your vacation?"

Ham shrugged but ambled up in front of Mrs. Volini's desk.

"I ate."

"What did you say?" Mrs. Volini asked incredulously.

"I ate. I spent my whole vacation eating."

"Kevin, don't exaggerate. It would be impossible to spend your whole vacation just eating."

"I slept, too. Oh, and I watched television."

The class was roaring by now, but Ham seemed puzzled by their laughter. "No, really. My grandmother visited us, and she's a great cook. She made these great cookies and chicken soup and blintzes, which are these dough things with cheese inside, and you eat them with sour cream or applesauce, only I ate them with both. . . ."

"Enough, Kevin," Mrs. Volini said through clenched teeth.

"All right." Ham sounded aggrieved. "But you asked."

Mrs. Volini looked sorry that she had. "What about you, Bobby?" She seemed to have forgotten about not volunteering people.

Gretchen admired the way Bobby easily rose and began speaking. She supposed if you were an actor, it was important that you didn't mind having people look at you.

"I was cast in a movie."

Now this was what everyone wanted to hear. Even Mrs. Volini leaned forward with interest.

"My agent heard that a movie called *The Pocket Pickers* was being filmed around here. The star is Greg Marsh. He was in *Psycho Man*." Whispers went around the classroom. Everyone had heard of Greg Marsh. "The movie's about a guy who takes street kids and makes them into a gang of pickpockets," Bobby continued. "They're a lot like Fagin's gang in *Oliver Twist*, if you know that book."

"How many have read *Oliver Twist*?" Mrs. Volini interrupted.

Several kids said they had seen the movie.

"It might be fun to read aloud to you. Go on, Bobby."

"Well, my agent sent me out on a casting call. That's where they choose people to be in the movie. I thought I was just going to be in a crowd scene or something, but I got chosen to be one of the pocket pickers. I have a couple of lines. Not too many." He went on to talk about the other people in the movie and where in town the shooting was going on.

"Will this affect your schoolwork, Bobby?" Mrs. Volini asked.

Gretchen could see Veronica, who sat across

from her, whispering to her best friend and shadow, Candy Dahl, "Who cares?" For once, Gretchen had to agree with her.

"I might have to take some time off, but there will be a tutor on the set. My mother is going to call you about it."

"This does all sound fascinating. You'll keep us posted on the moviemaking?"

"Sure, if you want me to."

"We certainly do."

Mrs. Volini called on Candy next, and even though Gretchen didn't like Candy, she felt a little sorry for her. Who would want to follow Bobby?

As Candy talked about her trip to Saint Louis, Gretchen smoothed and resmoothed her short hair. It was so weird. She had lost weight, gotten her hair cut, and tried so hard to look different because she was tired of being the class fatty. But now, when she had a legitimate opportunity to stand up in front of the class and show them what she had accomplished, she was too embarrassed to even consider it. If Mrs. Volini called on her, she'd probably have to get up and leave the room.

What was wrong with her? Here she was, the new, improved Gretchen Hubbard, and she didn't feel one bit better than she had before.

CHAPTER
THREE

"So what do you want to do?" Robin asked Gretchen as they walked together out of the school at the end of a long day.

"Go over to my house?" Gretchen suggested.

"No, we don't want to go home. We want to show you off."

Gretchen groaned. "I think everyone in school has already seen me."

"And they all thought you looked great."

"Well, they stared at me."

Gretchen had spent most of the day pretending she was invisible. She had learned the trick of being invisible when she was fat, and with so many kids looking at her today, she immediately put it back into practice.

It was easy, actually. First, you kept your head down, that was essential. Gretchen had done it for years. Sometimes she felt as if she knew every crack in the Kennedy Middle School corridors. Then, it was important to always be thinking hard about something. It could be schoolwork, your family, even the television show you saw the night before, but whatever the topic, you had to concentrate on that and nothing else to shut out the noise of the giggling and talking around you. But the number-one thing was, if some comments did penetrate your fog, and if they were about you, you just drew deeper inside yourself. You pretended that you weren't even there, and if you weren't there, you couldn't hear anything, of course. Then you scurried away as fast as possible.

When Gretchen used to dream about being thin, she'd assumed that once she had achieved her goal, she wouldn't have to pretend she was invisible anymore. But oddly enough, she had been doing it more today than she had in ages.

"I really just want to go home."

Robin brushed aside her protests. "No, you don't. We'll go to The Hut." She tried to look nonchalant. "Besides, I told Jon I'd be there."

Gretchen wavered. Maybe it would be all

right. "Okay. I can go for a little while, I guess."

"Good," Robin beamed. "Say," she added, digging around in her purse, "let's put on some of this." Triumphantly, she pulled out a lipstick still in its packaging.

"Robin! Are you allowed?"

Robin giggled. "Not really. But this is kind of special. First day back at school and all."

"First day of seeing Jon, you mean."

"Yeah," Robin replied, laughing a little harder now.

"My mother wasn't real happy when I had that makeup on," Gretchen reminded her.

"She's in Santa Fe. Besides, it's just a little lipstick." Robin was feeling daring, Gretchen could tell.

"When did you buy it?"

"Yesterday. You looked so great when that woman made you up." Robin shrugged. "Well, I just wanted to try some makeup, too. I had some money saved from my birthday. Oh, and I bought this." She reached down in her purse again and showed Gretchen a blusher in a case with a small brush and a little mirror.

"Robin!"

"Aw, I couldn't resist." Robin drew Gretchen over to a bus-stop shelter and plunked herself down on the bench. After ripping the packaging, she looked in the mirror and began applying the pink lipstick.

"What color is that?" Gretchen asked, a little alarmed. It was awfully pink.

"Passion Pansy." Robin eyed herself critically. "What do you think?"

Gretchen didn't know what to say. There was something about Robin's red hair, freckles, and Passion Pansy that didn't quite work together. Robin looked as if she was all lips. Heavy, pink clown lips.

Robin's smile faded. "Dopey, right?"

"Maybe it's not your color."

"Darn." Robin found a tissue in her pocket and began rubbing off the lipstick. "I couldn't try it on in the store. But the color looked so pretty on the package. Three-fifty, down the drain," she said with disgust.

"Sorry," Gretchen said, commiserating.

"Wait a minute." Robin held out the Passion Pansy. "I bet this would look great on you."

"You don't want me to try it on now?"

"Sure, why not?"

Reluctantly, Gretchen took the lipstick. Holding it as if it were a snake, she carefully opened it, brought it to her lips, and lightly applied it.

"Wow! I can't believe how different it looks on you." Robin passed her the mirror.

It was incredible. Where Robin looked like she had painted on a clown mouth, Gretchen's lips looked nice and pouty.

"Now the blusher," Robin insisted.

Gretchen was getting into this. She whisked the small brush back and forth on the blusher, shook off the excess, and carefully smoothed it on her cheeks.

"Gee, you do a good job," Robin said admiringly.

"I watched the girl in the department store."

"It's great! Too bad we don't have any eye makeup."

Gretchen snapped closed the blusher and pushed it over to Robin. "This is plenty. I think I'd better get home."

"What are you talking about? Now that you look so terrific, you have to go to The Hut."

Should she go? Lately, she always felt as if she was changing her mind: one minute she'd be sure she didn't want to do something, then she'd be positive the next minute that she did. "Oh, all right." She could stay for a little while and leave. There was something about wearing the makeup that made her feel daring, too.

The girls walked through downtown Forest

Glen. They passed several antiques shops and stopped to look in the windows of clothing stores. When they got to The Hut, it was already full.

The Hut really was kind of a shack where you could get the best hamburgers and hot dogs in town. It was a hangout for the middle-school kids and most of the junior-high students as well. Today, it seemed as if every kid from both schools had the idea to grab a Coke or have some fries before going home.

"Wow!" Robin said, looking around. "It's really crowded in here."

"Yeah. Do you see Jon?"

"No. I'll look around. Why don't you get us a couple of diet Cokes?" Robin suggested.

Gretchen went over to the crowded counter and waited to get her drinks. She was idly studying the menu, thinking about all the food she couldn't eat, when a voice behind her said, "What's good here?"

Whirling around, Gretchen saw a boy with tousled dark hair and brown eyes looking down at her. What she noticed most, though, was the dusting of freckles across his nose. He was at least fifteen, and he must be new in town, Gretchen figured, or else he'd know what to order. "Hot dogs are the best," she murmured.

40

"This is a pretty hot spot," the boy said. Then he frowned. "But most of the kids are so young. Except us, of course."

Us? What was this kid talking about? She was only twelve.

"Do you go to the high school here?"

Before she could answer, the girl behind the counter handed her the two colas. Relieved, Gretchen turned to go.

"Well, see you," the boy said.

"See you," Gretchen answered and hurried away, toward the table where she spotted Robin, Jonathan, and Ham.

When she arrived, Robin whispered, "Who was that boy you were talking to?"

Gretchen shrugged. "I don't know."

"I couldn't get a good look at him, but he seemed cute."

"He was old."

"What are you two whispering about?" Jonathan asked.

"Nothing," the girls said in unison.

"You girls," Ham said, and then slurped at his milk shake. "Always got some secrets." He glanced up at Gretchen. "Hey, what's that stuff on your face?"

"Lipstick." Gretchen left it at that. She wasn't sure Ham would even know what blusher was.

"Since when do you wear lipstick?"

Gretchen desperately wished someone would change the subject, and as if in answer to her unspoken plea, Robin said, "What do you think of that newspaper idea Mrs. Volini was talking about?"

"More work," Jon said, digging into his fries.

"But it sounded like fun," Robin argued.

"I'm going to be the editor."

All eyes swiveled in Ham's direction. Ham never wanted to do anything. He was notorious for getting his homework in late, and the last time anyone could remember his volunteering was in the fourth grade, when he took a hamster home over spring break. It died.

"Hey, what are you all staring at me for?"

"Since when are you interested in newspapers?" Jonathan asked.

"Since I've been reading one."

"I can't believe you know what a newspaper is," Robin teased.

Ham was beginning to look really miffed. "Maybe I wasn't always a big newspaper fan, but now we've got home delivery, and I read it every day."

"The comics?" Jon suggested.

Ham sat up straight. "The news and the

editorial pages. Why, the paper is full of interesting stuff."

Robin, Jon, and Gretchen looked at one another. This was a side of Ham Berger they'd never seen.

"So what makes you think Mrs. Volini is going to put you in charge of this project?" Jon asked.

" 'Cause I've got great ideas." He began ticking them off on his fingers. "We could have exposes. . . ." The way he said it the word rhymed with *noses*.

"Not exposes," Gretchen interrupted, "it's pronounced *expo-zays*."

"Whatever. Stories about why the showers in the gym never work right. And gossip. Like maybe we could find out if that new music teacher is dating anyone." Ham looked a little dreamy.

"Hey, Ham, I hate to burst your bubble, but I've heard other people saying they'd like to be in charge of the paper," Robin informed him. "Veronica, for one, was mentioning that to Candy."

"Those two," Ham snorted.

"Well, good luck," Jon said, "but I've got to tell you, Ham, I don't think it's too likely Mrs. Volini is going to choose you. You're not her favorite person, in case you haven't noticed."

"Yeah, I have," Ham said gloomily. "Remember before break she told me if I didn't clean up my desk, she was going to ask the janitor to put it and me in the big can in the boiler room?"

Jon punched Ham in the arm. "You might have trouble writing your exposes"—he deliberately mispronounced the word—"from in there."

Gretchen finished up her drink and glanced at the clock over the counter. "I think I'd better get going."

"I'm going to stay for a while," Robin said.

"That's all right. I'll take the bus home."

She gathered up her books, said good-bye to her friends, and headed out the door. As usual, her head was down, and she almost bumped into the boy she had been talking to earlier.

"I had my Coke out here," he said. "It's a great day."

She didn't know why, but she quoted a line from an old song her father used to sing to her. "Blue skies, smiling at me." Immediately, she was mortified. How could she have uttered such a ridiculous thing?

But to her amazement, the boy sang the next line, "Nothing but blue skies, do I see." He had a nice voice.

"You know it," she exclaimed.

"My dad's favorite."

"My dad's, too."

"Where are you headed?" he asked.

"Home." She didn't want to talk to this teenager. "Bye," she said as she left him standing there. The whole exchange had made her nervous.

By the time Gretchen arrived at her house, she had decided she was making a mountain out of a molehill. Chances were she'd never see this guy again. If anything, she should be flattered by his attention, but mostly it just felt weird.

Gretchen had come to hate walking into an empty house. When her mother lived at home, she was always back from the bank by three-fifteen, squirreled away in her attic office, working on one of her short stories. Since her mom had left, it was as if a heavy gray fog had filled up the house, one that you could get lost in.

Not that her dad didn't try. He owned a garage where he worked on fancy cars like Mercedes and Porsches, and because he was his own boss, he was usually home right at five. Before her mom had left, Gretchen and her dad had almost been strangers. Now they would at least fix dinner together and talk about how their days went.

Even though Gretchen didn't know anything about cars and didn't want to know anything about them, her dad could tell a story about how some salesman was trying to sell him a new kind of wrench and make it funny. Mr. Hubbard kept saying there ought to be a sitcom set in a garage.

They didn't talk too much about Mrs. Hubbard. Sometimes her dad acted as if he had completely forgotten who she was, and that made Gretchen mad.

If a letter arrived, he never read it until a couple of days later. When Gretchen came back from Santa Fe, her father had wanted to know all the details of her trip, but whenever her mother's name was mentioned, he seemed to change the subject. She had been telling her dad about the drive they had all taken up to Taos, and how Mrs. Hubbard had gotten lost, even though the road from Santa Fe went almost directly there. It was so funny because her mother had started giggling, and then she had to go to the bathroom, right there in the middle of nowhere. Gretchen had tried to make it a good story, like the kind her dad told, but all he had said was, "The mountains must have been pretty. What did they look like?"

Today she walked into the house and threw her books down on the hall table. To her surprise, her father was standing in the doorway of the kitchen. He was a nice-looking dad, as dads went, on the tall side, with sandy hair. The most noticeable thing about him was his smile, which seemed more shy than happy.

"What are you doing home so early, Dad?"

"I wanted to hear about your first day back. Did everyone like your new look?" he inquired.

"I guess." It was a good thing her father hadn't seen her in lipstick and blusher. She had managed to wipe off most of it on the bus ride home.

"I bet they thought you looked spectacular."

The boy at The Hut passed briefly through Gretchen's mind.

To change the subject, she told him about the class newspaper and Ham wanting to be the editor.

"What about homework? Do you have any?"

"Oh, yeah. I have a math assignment already."

"Maybe you should get to it while I fix dinner."

"All right. Was there any mail today?"

"You got a letter from your mother."

"Where is it?"

He gestured toward the little desk in the kitchen.

Gretchen hurried to get it. She ripped the envelope open and scanned the letter's contents quickly. Her mother said she missed Gretchen and she hoped to have news about her plans very soon.

Gretchen wondered if she should say something to her dad. Clearing her throat, she walked over to the counter, where he was chopping carrots for a salad. "Mom says hi," she began.

"Mmm."

Screwing up her courage, she said, "When I was in Santa Fe, I talked to her, Dad."

Her father wiped the knife. "About what?"

"Whether she's coming home. Last September, you guys said this was an experiment, for the school year. But now it seems like she might stay longer." Gretchen's voice faltered.

"She's got some decisions to make," Mr. Hubbard said noncommittally.

"Mom said she felt like she wanted to be in two places at once. I know she misses us."

"I'm sure she misses you."

"Both of us," Gretchen insisted.

Mr. Hubbard began chopping the lettuce.

"Don't you even want her to come home?" Gretchen burst out.

Her father didn't look up. "I think we've been doing all right on our own."

How should she answer that? They had been doing all right, but it wasn't the same. Not like when her mother was there. There were lots of things she was too embarrassed to talk about with her dad. Why, she'd just been praying she wouldn't get her period the way some of the girls had. She would die if she had to tell him she had cramps or something. Before Mrs. Hubbard went away, she had bought Gretchen the things she would need if it happened, but still . . . how could her dad not want her mother home?

"Dad, maybe if you wrote to her, told her to come home."

"That's her decision," he said tightly. "Why don't you get on that homework?"

Gretchen stomped off toward her bedroom. Why did everything have to be so complicated? She was finally thin, and still nothing seemed right.

C H A P T E R
FOUR

Gretchen was dreaming about a chocolate cake. A big luscious chocolate cake with short, fat chocolate arms was beckoning to her from the table. She was just about to take a bite when a telephone started ringing, and Gretchen started running all around trying to find it. Groggily she realized that the phone really was ringing. She opened her eyes and groped around, trying to find the telephone next to her bed.

"Hello?" she said in a sleepy voice.

"Gretchen, what are you doing?" Robin demanded.

Gretchen mumbled something about chocolate cake.

"At this hour?"

"What time is it?" Gretchen squinted at the clock on her bed stand.

"Eight-thirty."

"You're calling me at eight-thirty on a Saturday?"

"You've got to get up. We can go watch the shooting."

Gretchen was still foggy enough to have Robin's words conjure up an image of a firing squad. "What!"

"*The Pocket Pickers*. Bobby told Jon last night. They're doing a scene in Hudson Park."

Gretchen sat up. This was exciting. "Can just anyone go watch?"

"It's outside. There's not much to stop us."

"What time?"

"It's probably already started. Bobby had a really early call."

"Should I meet you at the park?"

"Yeah. Get there as fast as you can."

Gretchen hopped out of bed and ran downstairs. Her father usually went to the garage on Saturday mornings, but maybe, if he hadn't left yet, she could get a ride.

Mr. Hubbard was at the kitchen table, drinking a cup of coffee. Instead of reading the newspaper, as he usually did, he was writing a letter. He looked up a little guiltily as Gretchen came into the room.

"You're up early," he said.

Gretchen quickly filled him in on the movie-making.

"I can drop you off on my way to the garage if you hurry."

"Oh, I'm hurrying, all right." She hesitated. Was the letter to her mother? Should she ask? Maybe it was better just to leave the subject alone. "I'll be down as fast as I can," Gretchen said. Her dad seemed relieved and nodded.

"Clothes again," Gretchen groaned after taking the world's fastest shower. She had been in school for a week and had used up almost all her new outfits. This worrying about what to wear was something new in Gretchen's life, and she wasn't sure she liked it.

Finally she decided on a pair of black jeans and a long, black Chicago White Sox T-shirt with silver lettering. She was surprised at how good they looked; especially with her spiked hair.

"Okay, I'm ready," Gretchen said as she bounded down the stairs.

"What's with all the black?"

"Doesn't it look all right?" Gretchen immediately started to worry.

"Actually, it looks kind of sophisticated. I'm not used to seeing you in black."

"It was all I had clean."

Her father's face cleared. "Oh. I thought you were making some kind of statement."

"I was," Gretchen responded with a grin. "Time to do the wash."

By the time Gretchen arrived at Hudson Park, there were all sorts of people milling around. She had been concerned about finding the shoot, but with the cameras, lights, and trailers, there was no way she could have missed it. Now she just had to find her friends.

It was Robin who found her, though. "Where have you been? I think they're about to start."

"I can't believe this," Gretchen said, looking around wide-eyed.

"Right here in Forest Glen. Who would have thunk it? Sharon, Jon, and Ham are waiting by that tree. Let's get over there."

"Where's Bobby?" Gretchen asked when they joined the group.

"I haven't spotted him yet," Jon replied.

Sharon tugged on her arm. "But that's Greg Marsh, isn't it?"

Gretchen looked to where Sharon was pointing. She had seen Greg Marsh in lots of movies, but he was so far away, it was difficult to tell. This man had a beard and a close-cropped haircut. Still, it could be Greg Marsh.

"I don't think it's him," Robin argued.

"Maybe it's his stand-in," Jonathan suggested.

Gretchen squinted. Then someone else caught her eye. Over by the merry-go-round, reading what looked like a script, was the boy who had spoken to her at The Hut. He was in the movie!

"Hey, you kids are going to have to move behind that rope." A tall girl wearing a T-shirt that said "Pocket Pickers" began shooing them away.

"But we know someone in the movie," Ham objected.

"Don't we all," the girl said with an exaggerated sigh. "Behind the rope."

Grumbling, the kids moved. Now they were even farther away from the action. Gretchen tried to keep her eye on the boy, but he disappeared into a trailer.

Nothing happened for a long time. Jessica, who was in Mr. Jacobs's sixth-grade class, joined them. "When's it going to start?" she kept asking. After the third time, she started to get on everyone's nerves.

"We still don't know," Robin said.

"Bobby said moviemaking could be really boring," Jon informed them.

"Well, he was right," Robin replied. "We've been here for almost an hour, and people are just wandering around." She glanced over at Ham, who had been suspiciously silent through all their grumbling. "What are you doing?"

Ham flipped closed a little pocket notebook he had been writing in. "Taking notes."

"On what?"

Ham waved his arm expansively. "The excitement of the movies."

"It's not exciting, Ham," Jon said. "That's why we're all complaining."

"What are you going to do with the notes anyway?" Robin asked.

"I'm going to use them to write an article. Then Mrs. Volini will see that I should be the editor of the paper."

The kids looked at one another. What was with Ham?

"But what are you going to write?" Sharon asked. "Unless things get a lot more interesting, you've got a story that says movie people talk to each other and drink lots of coffee."

"Hey, I'm not telling." Ham clutched the notebook to his chest as if someone was going to take it away from him.

Ham was spared any more interrogation

when a voice came over a loudspeaker yelling, "We need quiet on the set now. Everybody take your places, please."

All the spectators, almost a hundred people by now, crowded against the rope. The boy from The Hut, Bobby, and several other kids settled themselves under a tree. Greg Marsh—it did seem to be him—stood in front of them.

Now all the frenzy simmered down. *"Pocket Pickers,"* a man with a clap-board called, "scene five, take one."

Gretchen strained to hear what the actors were saying, but they were too far away for her to make out much of the dialogue. Greg Marsh seemed to be talking about a rich old woman and how they could get friendly with her. The boy from The Hut said, "Here we go again," and the man sitting up above them on some sort of camera contraption called, "Cut." Then the actors relaxed.

"That's it?" Gretchen asked, disappointed.

The kids waited a few minutes, and then the same scene started all over again. Same words, same motions.

"Well, it's kind of fun to see Greg Marsh," Gretchen said uncertainly.

"Barely see him, you mean," Robin replied.

Jon looked at his watch. "I think the high-

56

school kids play ball on the other side of the park about now. Maybe I'll go over there."

"They're doing it once more," Robin said, gesturing toward the group at the tree.

"Well, I don't want to see it a third time," Sharon said with disgust. "I'm going home to get ready for my ballet lesson."

"I'll walk with you," Jessica said.

"What about you, Ham?" Jon asked.

Ham was still busily writing in his notebook. "I'm gonna stay."

"Do you want to watch the ball game with me?" Jon said, looking sideways at Robin.

Robin glanced at Gretchen.

"I'm going to the . . . library," Gretchen said. There was nothing she needed to do there, but the last thing she wanted was to be a third wheel.

Pulling Gretchen to the side, Robin whispered, "You can come. We're only going to watch some high schoolers play baseball."

"No. I want to get started on that English assignment anyway." She hoped she sounded convincing.

"All right then."

Gretchen watched as Robin and Jonathan wandered off.

"Hey, Gretchen?"

"What, Ham?" She turned to him.

"What color would you say those pants are?"

"Whose pants?"

"The ones the pocket pickers are wearing."

Gretchen raised an eyebrow. "They're blue, Ham. Just like all blue jeans."

"I knew that," Ham said, exasperated. "But I wanted to write down exactly what color they are. Like sky blue or navy blue . . ."

"Blue-jean blue," Gretchen said and turned to leave the park.

Walking to the library gave Gretchen too much time to think. Why was she all by herself on such a beautiful spring Saturday? Not that she was jealous of Robin—oh, maybe she was a little bit—but it didn't seem fair that everyone but her had something to do.

When she finally got there, Gretchen wondered if she should go in. She loved the library, but being there on a day like today reminded her too much of her formerly fat life.

Not that she minded reading. Actually, one of the okay things about being lonely was that it gave you time to read lots of good books. But she didn't feel like picking out books today, even though she was feeling plenty lonely. Maybe she should just trudge over to her dad's garage and go home.

Suddenly she was famished. She glanced at

one else believed it, too. A few moments later, Candy swung through the door. Her face lit up when she saw Veronica, who immediately started whispering to her as soon as the two girls sat down.

Hanging her head, Gretchen knew that she and her lunch were the subject under discussion. She didn't even want the stupid hot dog now, but if she pushed it aside, Veronica would think Gretchen was taking her oh-so-well-intentioned advice.

Without turning to see if Veronica and Candy were watching, Gretchen took a big bite of her hot dog. She waited for that familiar rush she used to get as her taste buds sent a message to her brain: "Hey! Good stuff! Have some more!" But as she chewed, she realized the hot dog didn't taste so terrific after all. It was getting a little cold, and the greasy flavor was pronounced. Maybe it was because she was used to yogurt and salads, but Gretchen had the feeling if she ate the whole meal in front of her, she would wind up feeling as though someone had dropped a bowling ball in the pit of her stomach.

Veronica or no, it was clear to Gretchen that she didn't want this food. She was about to pick up the tray and dump it in the trash when she felt another tap on her shoulder.

"Veron—oh, it's you." Gretchen was looking up into the brown eyes of the boy in the movie.

"I guess this is the place to find you," he said.

Tongue-tied, Gretchen just nodded. It had been hard enough to speak to this guy when she didn't know he was an actor, but now she couldn't open her mouth.

"Can I sit down?" he asked, apparently not noticing her silence.

"Sure," Gretchen squeaked.

"Don't you want your hot dog?"

Gretchen shook her head.

"Mind if I eat it?"

"It's getting cold."

"I don't care." To prove it, he took a giant bite. "So what's your name anyway?"

"Gretchen." She screwed up her courage and said, "What's yours?"

"Tim. Tim Columbo."

"You're in that movie, right?"

Tim seemed surprised she knew. "Yeah," he said, taking some fries. "We're on a break, and I didn't feel like eating the food in the lunch wagon."

"Lunch wagon?"

"The film company brings in food in those open trucks, and the cast and crew have to line up to get it. I'm not due back for a while, so I thought I'd come over here and get one of those great hot dogs you recommended." He smiled at her, and Gretchen felt as though The Hut had just put in new, brighter lighting.

There were a million things she wanted to ask him, but she didn't know if she should. Or could. There were butterflies beating a hard tattoo in her stomach.

"Say, want to wait while I have a dog of my own? Then you can show me this town."

The butterflies turned into elephants. "I . . . can't. I have to get home." Clumsily, she pushed away from the table.

"Okay." Tim's expression turned bored. "Whatever."

"Sorry," she mumbled as she turned to leave.

By the time she was outside, the elephants were joined by horses stomping on her heart. She had never heard it beating so loudly.

Gretchen wasn't out the door two seconds when Veronica and Candy came flying out behind her.

"Candy says that boy is in the movie. Is that true?" Veronica demanded.

"Yes."

"Well, what in the world was he doing talking to you?" Candy asked bluntly.

Gretchen glared at her. Candy Dahl thought she was so great. She was nothing but Veronica's stupid lackey. And now, Gretchen realized, Candy was chubbier than she was. It gave Gretchen courage. "He was asking me out."

"Oh, in your dreams," Candy said disgustedly.

"It's true," Gretchen replied. Showing him around town would have been a kind of date.

Veronica took the highroad. "Come on, Gretchen, that kid . . ."

"Tim," Gretchen interjected.

Veronica looked surprised. "Tim. Anyway, he's got to be fifteen, maybe sixteen. What would he want with you?"

"I don't know," Gretchen said honestly.

"I don't believe you for a second." Candy shook her head as if to emphasize her point.

"Me either," Veronica said.

"Who cares? It's true."

"Well, are you going?" Veronica asked.

"No."

She began to walk away, but she could hear Veronica and Candy whispering as they followed her.

The girls caught up to her, one on either side. "If he really asked you out, you could get him to do it again," Veronica said smoothly.

Gretchen kept walking. "Why would I do that?"

"To prove you're not a liar," Candy said. "Otherwise, we'd have to tell everyone you are."

Fear stabbed Gretchen. Who would believe her if she said Tim asked her out?

"Look, we'll make a bet with you," Veronica interrupted.

Stopping short, Gretchen asked, "What's the bet?"

"You get Tim to ask you out again, and I'll . . ." She thought for a moment. "I'll give you this sweatshirt." It was a great-looking gray sweatshirt with "Harvard" stamped on the front.

"And we won't tell anyone you're a liar," Candy added smugly.

"But if I win," Veronica said, "you have to let me copy your math homework for a week."

"We'll get in trouble."

"No, we won't, because if you're telling the truth, you'll win the bet," Veronica said with a smirk.

This is stupid, Gretchen told herself. But she wanted to prove something to these two. For years they had made fun of her, called her every fat name they could think of. Tim had seemed interested in her. It shouldn't be too hard to get him to ask her out. Then Veronica and Candy would know she wasn't the same Hippo Hubbard they had used as a punching bag. She'd show them.

Breathing heavily, she shook on the bet.

As she trudged toward her father's garage, she tried to feel elated. This was her big moment.

"Oh, my gosh," she said aloud. "What have I done?"

CHAPTER
FIVE

Gretchen sat in the middle of the mall, looking at all the people hurrying by. She hoped she hadn't missed Robin, though it didn't seem possible that she could have. She had arrived fifteen minutes early.

Yesterday had turned into a long afternoon and evening. She could hardly believe that she had made such a stupid bet. She tried hard not to think about it, starting her homework as soon as she arrived home. So intent had she been on finishing her math, English, and history that finally her father had stuck his head in the door and said, "Don't you want to take a bike ride or something? It's quite a nice day, and you've missed most of it."

"Not really," Gretchen had replied, chewing her pencil and trying to look as though she was deep in concentration. "I have to get this done."

She knew she couldn't drag the homework out all evening, though, so it was a relief when the next-door neighbors called and asked her to baby-sit for their two-and-a-half-year-old daughter. Gretchen baby-sat just a little, and she suspected that the Mandevilles only called her when they absolutely couldn't get anyone else. Even then, they always checked with her father to make sure he was going to be home in case some dire emergency required adult help. They didn't pay much either, but this night Gretchen would have paid them for a chance to get out of the house. She knew she wouldn't be able to think about her own problems with Jamie running around, her diaper falling down around her ankles.

The evening had been as raucous and time-consuming as she'd hoped until Jamie went to bed. But once the house was quiet, Gretchen lay down on the couch and stared at a dirty spot on the wall. She supposed, bottom line, she should be happy about all this newfound attention, but it also made her mad. Tim would never have looked at her twice a year ago. Now here he was causing all sorts of problems.

She would have liked to call Robin and tell her everything that had happened, but she knew that the Millers were going over to a relative's to celebrate an anniversary. She and Robin had already made plans to meet at the mall the next day, so Gretchen could fill her in then. Gretchen had finally zapped on the TV, hoping she could find something interesting to distract her, but the airwaves seemed filled with game shows about dating and making love connections.

Now, with the mall traffic getting more frenzied by the moment, Gretchen again glanced impatiently at the wristwatch her mother had gotten her for her last birthday. It was two minutes later than the last time she looked.

Glancing down the long corridor, she thought she saw Robin's red hair off in the distance. She kept her eyes trained on the girl as she came closer. Gretchen finally decided it was Robin. But who was that walking alongside her? "Oh, no," Gretchen moaned. "Veronica."

Robin looked a little embarrassed as she came up to Gretchen with Veronica right behind her. "Hi," she said quietly.

"Hi."

"Veronica called me this afternoon and asked if she could come with us."

Why did you say yes? Gretchen wondered silently.

Even Veronica looked contrite. "It had been a long time since Robin and I had done anything together," she explained. "And you and I . . ."

"We've never done anything together."

Veronica looked surprised that Gretchen would talk back to her like that.

"I tried to call you, but you'd already left," Robin added apologetically.

"What's the big deal?" Veronica said. "So I'm here, so what?"

Gretchen ignored Veronica. Turning to Robin, she said, "She's just here to make fun of me."

Robin looked unhappy but didn't say anything.

Why couldn't Robin see what Veronica was up to? "If you don't believe me, ask her about that stupid bet she made with me yesterday."

"Hey, I didn't force you to bet," Veronica replied, tossing her dark hair over her shoulder. "You really thought you could get that boy to ask you out, so I wanted you to prove it."

Robin looked at Gretchen in amazement. "What boy? What bet?"

Trying to sidestep Veronica's interruptions, Gretchen told Robin the whole story.

"Gretchen, you don't know anything about this guy," Robin fretted. She sat down heavily on the bench.

"So? He was nice," Gretchen replied defiantly.

"But if he knew how old you are . . ."

"Well, he doesn't," she snapped.

Robin stared at her. They had never had a fight before. Veronica just looked on, smiling slightly.

"Besides, who said I was actually going on the date?"

"Now wait a minute," Veronica began.

"Uh-uh. We bet that he'd ask me out. That was it."

Now it was Gretchen's turn to smile as Veronica's face took on a defeated expression. Finally Veronica mumbled, "He won't even do that."

"We'll see," Gretchen said almost gaily. She felt as though she had won a round.

"If you're not going out with him I guess that's different," Robin said. "I can't wait to see him again." She grew more excited. "I just caught a glimpse of him at The Hut. He's really handsome, huh?"

"Ask Veronica," Gretchen said.

"Yeah, he's handsome. Are we going to shop or what?"

Gretchen and Robin exchanged looks. Maybe this shopping expedition wouldn't be too bad after all. Not if they could keep Veronica off balance.

"Do we actually have any money?" Robin asked, as they strolled along.

"I do." Veronica pulled out her wallet and flashed two twenty-dollar bills.

"Your mother gives you that much to spend?" Gretchen said, surprised. "On whatever you want?"

"Well, I am supposed to be looking for shoes," Veronica reluctantly replied.

"Oh, shoes." Gretchen's father let her buy shoes, too. It was hard to waste money on those.

"I spent the rest of my birthday money on that makeup," Robin said regretfully. "What do you have, Gretchen?"

She fingered the fifteen dollars that were crumpled in a ball in her pocket. Ten dollars had been around since Christmas, and the rest was left over from her trip to Santa Fe. Gretchen had had a vague idea about buying something new to wear for when she ran into Tim again, but with Veronica around, she didn't know if she wanted to shop for anything now.

"Do you have money?" Veronica asked, enunciating each word as if Gretchen were a little slow.

"Yes," Gretchen finally said.

"Well, how much?"

"Fifteen dollars."

"Great," Veronica said, pasting a phony smile on her face. "Then let's look for something for *you*."

Gretchen followed Veronica to first one store and then another, as if she were walking through a bad dream. Probably for Robin's benefit, Veronica was acting like a concerned friend, holding up blouses and cotton sweaters that she said would look great on Gretchen. Most of them resembled maternity tops.

"This has elephants on it," Gretchen said through gritted teeth as she caught a sweatshirt Veronica had tossed at her.

"So?" Veronica said innocently. "They're cute. I'd wear it."

Not if you had been compared to every fat creature in the animal kingdom, Gretchen thought to herself.

Robin took it away from Gretchen and looked at it critically. "It is cute." Then she glanced at the thundercloud that was

Gretchen's face. "But maybe it's not for you."

"The stuff we've been looking at really isn't sexy enough," Veronica agreed.

"Sexy? I don't want to look sexy."

"But you have all the requirements," Veronica said, looking at Gretchen's chest.

"Why don't we look for your shoes now?" Robin quickly interjected, trying to make peace.

"Oh, all right," Veronica said with a sigh.

As Veronica tried on every pair of flats in the Fancy Feet shoe store, Gretchen pulled Robin aside. "Why did you say she could come?"

"First she asked me about a homework assignment, then she started talking about her father's getting married again, and how her mom was depressed about it. She said she had to get out of the house."

"Couldn't she go for a walk or something?" Gretchen asked bitterly. She knew that Veronica hated the idea that her father was marrying a much younger woman, but she wondered if Veronica was only using this as an excuse to get back in Robin's good graces.

"I said I was busy, but she asked if she could come." Robin shrugged helplessly. "It's not like Veronica to beg."

Gretchen didn't like the fact that Robin was

still able to feel sorry for Veronica. "She's not coming to your house for dinner, is she?"

"No, of course not."

"Good, because if she was, I'd go home."

Later, up in Robin's pristine pink and white bedroom, Gretchen tried to explain why. "She just ruined everything, didn't you think?"

Robin thought about that as she sprawled over her bed. "She wasn't actually mean to you. Not like she used to be."

"No. Instead of calling me hippo to my face, she tossed elephants at me."

"I just wanted to give her a chance, Gretchen. Hey, nobody knows better than me how horrible she can be. But she can be fun, too . . . when she's being nice."

"When's that? Every other Columbus Day?"

Robin laughed. "Probably."

"Besides," Gretchen grumbled, "look at how much trouble she got me into with that stupid bet."

"Oh, Gretchen, it was stupid, but you didn't have to agree to it. I don't understand why you did."

Gretchen was sitting on Robin's floor, her legs crossed under her. For a long moment, she just picked at her jeans. Then she said, "I'm thin now, right?"

Robin nodded.

"But I don't feel thin, not really."

"What do you mean?" asked Robin. "You look skinnier every day."

"Remember in Santa Fe when you put on your bathing suit? You asked me if you looked fat. You!"

"In that two-piece, you can see this little roll around my stomach." Robin grabbed at it through her shirt. "The models in the magazines never have that."

"No kidding." How many models had she looked at with a combination of jealousy and dread? "But, Robin, if you can feel fat when you've been thin your whole life, imagine how I feel."

Robin lowered her voice. "I'm afraid I might wind up looking like my mom."

Mrs. Miller was ample, there was no question about that. Cooking was her hobby, and it showed.

"Well, I'm afraid I might start looking like me." Gretchen paused. "Robin, in my head I still do."

"You don't in Tim's," Robin replied. "Of course, he never saw you when you were overweight."

"You've got that right," Gretchen said a little resentfully. "Boys don't pay attention to fat girls. It makes me mad. I'm the same person after all."

"That's just the way things are, Gretchen."

"Not always. Your dad's crazy about your mom."

Robin made a face. "That's different. They're parents."

Mrs. Miller's voice announced dinner from downstairs. "Be right down," Robin yelled back. "So," she said, refocusing her attention on Gretchen, "you're going through with this."

"I think so," Gretchen said a little hesitantly.

"It's just a stupid bet."

"I know. But I'm hoping . . ." She stopped.

"What?"

"I don't know. If I can win this bet, maybe this new, improved Gretchen will seem real to me."

Before Robin could answer, Mrs. Miller called them again, a bit impatiently this time.

Mr. and Mrs. Miller were already sitting at the dining-room table by the time Robin and Gretchen got downstairs.

" 'O sole mio," Mr. Miller sang. "You're late for lasagn-a. We couldn't wait-a."

Mrs. Miller gave him a mock hit in the arm. Why couldn't all families be like the Millers? Gretchen wondered. She had once asked Robin how it was that her parents got along so well. Robin shrugged and said, "You should see them when they go at it." But from Gretchen's perspective, they always seemed to be joking around and having a good time.

"Gretchen," Mrs. Miller said apologetically, "I forgot about your diet. I hope that lasagna is all right. You know me, I'm afraid I always just make the most fattening thing."

"It's fine," Gretchen said. "I'll just take a small piece. I can fill up on the salad." And skip the garlic bread, she added to herself. She looked longingly at the long loaf, cut open and oozing butter.

"Well, I certainly give you credit," Mrs. Miller said, cutting the requested small square of lasagna. "I can't seem to lose a pound to save my soul. Not like these two skinny Minnies," she added, gesturing to her husband and Robin.

Gretchen wondered if she was going to spend her whole life eating small pieces of stuff. Was it worth it just to have boys like Tim noticing her?

"I'm going to make some coffee," Mrs. Miller said when everybody was finishing up. "Will you girls clear the table and load the dishwasher?"

"Oh, Mom," Robin groaned.

"Sure we will," Gretchen said hurriedly. She didn't want to seem like a bad guest.

"Thank you, Gretchen." Mrs. Miller gave Robin a look that said, Get up and start helping.

"Boy, I hate getting stuck with this job," Robin complained after the girls were in the kitchen, scraping the garbage into the disposal.

"Yeah, that's one way I keep myself from eating too much. I think of it as potential garbage."

"Oh, yuck," Robin said, scraping faster.

"It works."

Robin leaned toward Gretchen and whispered, "Sometimes I do wish my mother would go on a diet. She's a lot heavier than any of the other moms."

"But she's so nice."

"When I was best friends with Veronica, I always compared my mom to Mrs. Volner."

"There's no comparison. Mrs. Volner may be skinny and wear great clothes, but she always looks like she swallowed a lemon."

Robin laughed. "Sometimes."

Gretchen looked up at the kitchen clock. It was almost time for her to go home. "Before I call my dad to pick me up, let's call Bobby."

"Bobby Glickman? What for?"

"You know. I want him to give Tim my telephone number." Gretchen's voice was determined.

"All right, all right. We're just about done here. Let's go up to my room; we can phone from there."

"Say, Robin," Gretchen began as they climbed the stairs.

"No way!"

"How do you know what I'm going to ask?"

"You want me to talk to Bobby, don't you?"

"You know him better than I do," Gretchen argued.

When they got to her room, Robin handed Gretchen the phone. "I don't even think I agree with what you're doing. Letting you call from my phone is as far as I'm going to get involved."

"Will you at least give me his number?"

Reluctantly Robin looked it up in her address book.

Gretchen waited nervously as the phone rang in the Glickman house. She prayed that Bobby's mother wouldn't answer.

"Hello?" Bobby said.

Gretchen sighed with relief. "Bobby, it's Gretchen."

"Oh, hi."

There was a silence that Gretchen knew she needed to fill. "How's the movie going?"

"Pretty good. You were out there yesterday, right?"

"Did you see me?"

"No, Jon said you guys were there."

"Yeah, we were." More empty air. "Bobby?" Gretchen took a breath. "There's a guy in your movie. His name is Tim?" She glanced over at Robin, who was pretending to file her nails.

Bobby's voice became cautious. "Yeah, I know him."

"Well, the thing is, I know him, too."

"You do?"

"I met him. And he asked for my phone number, but I didn't give it to him. I sort of forgot, but I thought you could. Give it to him, that is."

Now the silence was on Bobby's end. "He's a teenager, Gretchen."

"Yeah, that's another thing. If you give him the number, I don't want him to know I'm in your class."

"Hey, this is getting complicated," Bobby objected.

Gretchen knew that. She could feel her palms beginning to sweat. "Bobby, all I am asking is that you give him my phone number and just tell him I'm a neighbor or something. Please."

"Okay, okay. But that's all I'm doing."

"Thanks, Bobby, I really appreciate it." Quickly she gave him her phone number, thanked him again, and hung up. "I'm glad that's over," she said with relief.

Robin threw down her nail file. "Over? It's just beginning."

CHAPTER
SIX

"The right to a free press shall not be abridged," Mrs. Volini read from the sixth-grade history book. "Can anyone tell me what that means?"

A boy named Jason raised his hand. "The newspapers can write anything they want?" he suggested.

"Well, yes, that's true, up to a point. Robin?"

"But you can't tell lies about people."

"Correct. A lie told in print about someone is called libel. Can anyone tell me why the framers of the Constitution thought it was so important that we have a free press? Kevin, you seem particularly eager to answer this question."

Ham stood up. "A free press is the corner-stone of a free society. Without the right of newspapers to print varying points of view, freedom would perish."

Mrs. Volini looked as if she was about to perish. "Kevin, how did you know that?"

"I read it in a book," Ham said seriously. "I memorized it."

"Well, you're certainly on top of this discussion."

Ham tried to look modest. "Yes. As a future journalist, I thought I should do some extra reading."

Gretchen sat close enough to Veronica to hear her mumble under her breath, "Oh, yeah, a regular Ted Koppel."

Mrs. Volini leaned forward. "Why, Kevin, I had no idea you wanted to be a journalist when you grow up."

Just the thought of Ham being grown up was frightening enough, Gretchen mused.

Ham gave a fake little chuckle. "Actually, I hoped I might get started earlier than that."

"You mean on our class newspaper." Mrs. Volini was so pleased her face was shiny.

Ham nodded earnestly.

"I was going to read a little more about freedom of the press, and then I thought we'd choose jobs." She looked up at the clock. "But it's almost time for lunch, so perhaps we can get to it immediately after our return. Be thinking about what role you'd like to play in our new adventure."

As the kids streamed toward the lunchroom, Gretchen looked around for Bobby. He hadn't been in class earlier, but with his movie schedule, sometimes he just showed up in the middle of the day. Nervously she wondered if he had passed on her message to Tim—and if he had done it the way she told him to. Boys didn't pay attention to important details the way girls did.

"I brought my lunch today," Robin said in her ear. "I'll grab a table."

"All right." Gretchen got a tray and pushed it down the counter. The one time she had no trouble watching what she ate was in the school cafeteria. Looking at the mystery meat congealing in fat, Gretchen felt like she could happily be on a diet forever. She took a container of yogurt and a banana and didn't feel deprived at all.

Scanning the room, looking for Robin, Gretchen caught sight of Bobby sitting with Jonathan, Ham, and a couple of other guys. She wanted desperately to go up and talk to him, but she didn't have the nerve. Not with all those boys around.

A horrible thought struck her. What if they were talking about her? She hadn't told Bobby not to tell about her and Tim. Of course, she just assumed he knew not to say anything. But that was silly. She doubted if Bobby had considered her privacy at all.

"Robin," she began as she put her tray down on the table, "I've got to talk to Bobby."

"He's here?" Robin said.

"Yes, he must have gotten to school just in time for lunch."

Robin took a bite of her bologna sandwich. "So go talk to him."

"Robin, he's sitting with all the boys."

Before Robin could answer, Veronica, Candy, and two of their friends, Kim and Natalie, came up with their trays. "Can we sit down?"

Robin and Gretchen exchanged glances. Usually girls were trying to sit at Veronica's table. Before either one of them could answer, Veronica sat down, and the other girls followed.

Gretchen was afraid that Veronica was going to bring up their bet, so she quickly asked, "So what about this newspaper thing?"

"What about it?" Veronica asked coolly.

"Are you going to try for any particular job?" Robin said.

"Editor-in-chief."

"Then she'll make me gossip editor," Kim said.

"Coeditor," Natalie corrected her. Kim and Natalie, with their short, swingy dark hair, looked almost exactly alike. They thought alike, too.

"You may have some competition, Veronica," Robin noted.

Veronica jerked her head up from her sandwich. "You want to be editor?"

"Not me. Ham."

"Oh, Ham." Veronica dismissed him with a wave of her hand. "He'd be a terrible editor. He's so disorganized."

"He can never find his homework," Kim added. "How could he put a newspaper together?"

"When he does his homework at all," Candy mumbled through a bite of sandwich.

"I don't know," Robin said. "Mrs. Volini seemed awfully impressed with him today."

"Not enough to make him editor." Veronica turned to Gretchen. "You're awfully quiet."

Gretchen shrugged.

"Any news from the wonderful world of moviemaking?"

The other girls, except Robin, looked around

and giggled. It was apparent they all knew about the bet.

"I didn't think you were going to tell everyone," Robin said.

"She didn't. I did." Candy smiled. "I was there, too, remember."

Gretchen finally found her voice. "Thanks a lot."

Veronica tilted her head and looked positively virtuous. "I told Candy you wouldn't like it."

Yeah, and probably laughed the whole time, Gretchen thought. "But you didn't tell her not to tell."

"Hey, I've got a mind of my own," Candy said indignantly.

The whole table broke up at that, even Veronica. If Candy had a mind of her own, it had never been noticeable before.

"Well, I have," Candy muttered.

Despite her dislike of Candy, Gretchen felt a little sorry for her. She knew how it was to be the butt of a joke. Why was it always the heaviest kid who seemed to get that distinction? Now Candy was the plumpest girl in the sixth grade. She dressed cool, and her big blue eyes and gold curls helped with the overall effect, but Gretchen had noticed that as her own weight had gone down, there had been a subtle shift in the way the kids treated Candy—lots more teasing, with plenty of the jokes centered on her name.

The worst had been when the class had been discussing the donation each sixth-grade class made to Kennedy before it went on to junior high school. Usually this meant choosing something to sell, and Mrs. Volini had suggested chocolate bars. Then Jason had yelled out, "No candy, please! We've got more than enough Candy to go around."

Everyone had laughed. Even Candy had tried to keep a smile on her face, but Gretchen knew she was dying inside. Since Candy had been one of her chief tormentors, Gretchen didn't know why she should waste a second feeling sorry for her, but she did. Maybe you always felt sorry for another fat person even if you didn't get along.

"So has the date been set up yet?" Veronica asked insistently, when the laughter over Candy and her missing mind had subsided.

"I'll let you know when it is."

Veronica just smiled.

As the topic at the table turned to other matters, Robin leaned over and whispered to Gretchen, "Bobby's up at the counter . . . alone."

Gretchen craned her neck. "Now or never, I guess."

She got up and went over to where Bobby was buying some milk. "Hi," she said tentatively.

"Oh, hi."

Gretchen guessed she'd have to ask. "So," she began, trying to sound casual, "did you see Tim today?"

"Yeah, I saw him." Putting her out of her misery, he said, "I gave him your phone number."

"And you didn't tell him I was in your class?" she asked anxiously.

"No, I said you were a neighbor."

"Well, I am, sort of."

"You live about two miles away."

"Everything's relative. Anyway, I appreciate it." She turned to go. Then she remembered the most important part. "Did he say he was going to call?"

Bobby shrugged. "All he said was 'thanks.'"

Thanks, that sounded promising anyway.

As Gretchen was walking back to the table, Ham stopped her. "Hey, Gretchen, I'm taking a kind of survey. If Mrs. Volini asks the class to vote on an editor, will you vote for me?"

"If it's between you and Veronica, sure. Besides, I liked what you said today. Did you ever finish that article on the movies?"

"Yeah, I gave it to Mrs. Volini right before we left for lunch."

Gretchen and Ham were interrupted by a shriek coming from a nearby table of fourth-grade girls.

"Something moved on this meat," a pony-tailed kid cried.

"No, it didn't," her friend replied. "That was just some grease running down it."

"Gross," another fourth grader said. "I think I'm going to be sick."

"Boy, I can't wait to get back to my yogurt," Gretchen told Ham.

"Yogurt's pretty disgusting, too. All white and slimy. Once when I had a cold . . ."

"Don't say it, Ham," Gretchen warned. She wondered if Mrs. Volini knew just what a way Ham had with words.

When they returned to the classroom after lunch, Mrs. Volini seemed as eager to get the newspaper going as Ham did. After they discussed freedom of the press for a while longer, she said, "Let's get started on our paper. The first person we must choose is the editor. The editor will shape the direction of the paper and make assignments. Does anyone wish to volunteer for the job?"

Both Ham and Veronica waved their hands in the air.

"Just the two of you? Well, why don't you both come up and tell us your vision of the newspaper."

Ham and Veronica came up to the front of the room. Before Ham could open his mouth, she stepped forward.

Veronica was never nervous in front of an audience. "I think our newspaper should tell the kids about what's happening at Kennedy Middle School. We should report on the activities of the students and the teachers." She glanced over at Ham. "The person who is chosen to be editor should be a well-organized person. Neat," she emphasized. "She should be a person who is well known and well thought of at Kennedy. Thank you," she added.

"All right, what about you, Kevin?" Mrs. Volini asked.

Ham looked off into space. "I see our newspaper as doing more than just reporting the facts. We want to get the stories behind the stories. That's what the best newspapers do, and that's why they are so important. They don't just tell people what's happening, they tell them why it's happening."

Mrs. Volini beamed at Ham, the second

time in one day. Then a worried look replaced her smile. "But, Kevin, you've never taken much interest in any of our class projects before."

That was a polite way to put it, Gretchen thought.

"I know," Ham replied seriously. "I guess I've just been waiting for something to grab me." The words sounded fine, but unfortunately Ham chose to punctuate his statement by grabbing his neck. He looked as if he were trying to choke himself, and the class roared.

"Please, children," a distressed Mrs. Volini said.

"I wasn't trying to be funny," Ham added, scowling.

Mrs. Volini stared at him for a few seconds. "No, I realize that."

While the class calmed down, Mrs. Volini made up her mind. "Veronica, you are certainly well qualified to be our editor, but I feel Kevin is more in tune with how our newspaper ties into our study of the First Amendment. So I think I will appoint Kevin Berger."

Veronica stomped back to her desk. Mrs. Volini put her arm across Ham's shoulder. "Now those of you who would like to be reporters or editors please gather at the back of the room. Any of you with particular artistic talents who'd like to be artists, cartoonists, or photographers come up here to the front. Businesspeople, those who will sell or promote the newspaper, over in the corner near the bulletin board. Ham will meet with your groups and hear your ideas."

By the time Gretchen got to the back of the room, there was already a large group of would-be writers and editors, Robin, Veronica, Candy, Kim, Sharon, and Jonathan among them. Veronica was already grumbling.

"I can't believe she picked the hamburger."

"Oh, give him a chance," Jon said.

"Well, he'd better make me fashion editor," she announced, "or he really is going to be ground meat."

"Why should you be fashion editor?" Sharon asked. "I wanted to be that."

Veronica gave her the once-over. "How optimistic of you."

Jon whispered to Jason, who was standing behind him, "I guess we don't have to worry about getting on the sports page."

"I hope I'll still get to be gossip editor," Kim said.

"It is what you do best," Robin replied, trying to keep a straight face.

The bickering continued until Ham, finished with the artists and cartoonists, came up to them. "All right," he said heartily, "here's my staff of reporters, ready to dig out the really good stories."

The kids looked at him dubiously.

"We already know what jobs we want," Veronica informed him.

Ham held up his hand. "No, I want to do this my way. I'm the editor. Now for sports, I think . . . Veronica."

"What!" Veronica, Jon, and Jason all yelped at the same time.

Gretchen and Robin looked at each other and rolled their eyes.

"I don't know a thing about sports," Veronica hissed.

"That's just it, Veronica. You can look at the whole thing with a fresh eye. Anyone can report scores, but because you don't really know anything about anything, you'll dig deeper, tell us why our teams are usually so bad. Is it the coaching staff? Poor equipment? See, you can find out. Now, Robin," he said, turning toward her, "I see you in the style section."

"What's that?" she asked warily.

"It's about having style," Kim answered for him. "And you don't have any."

"Well, she may not have much," Ham agreed, "but I also see it as a place to report trends. I think Robin would be great at that."

Robin looked a bit mollified.

"Jon, how about you and Jason teaming up for the gossip page?"

"You're nuts, you know that, Berger?" Jon looked ready to land a punch.

"Think about it. We always hear girls' gossip. What are the boys talking about?"

"Ham, what's *with* you?" Sharon asked with disgust.

Ham pointed to his nose.

"What? You've got a cold? It's affecting your thinking?"

"No," Ham said indignantly. "I've got a nose for news."

"This is what they must mean by no news is good news," Veronica said loudly.

Mrs. Volini heard her and came over. "Is there some problem here?"

"Ham—I mean Kevin's making all these weird assignments," Veronica informed her. "He's put me on sports."

"I'm just trying to get a fresh perspective."

Looking doubtful, Mrs. Volini said, "I'm sure you are, Kevin, but . . ." She started to say something and then apparently changed her mind. "Veronica, Kevin is in charge. We will do it his way."

Now it was Ham's turn to beam at Mrs.

Volini. "Okay, now on the light side, what about an astrology column?"

Gretchen stared at the phone. There was no reason it should ring. Just because Tim had her phone number didn't mean he was going to use it immediately. He might not call until tomorrow. Or never, a voice in her head intoned.

She lay back on her bed and wondered if she should start her math homework. But she didn't want to start it in case Tim called. She decided to put it off for a while. Closing her eyes, she tried to think of a story for the newspaper.

With everyone else getting such awful assignments, she felt a little guilty that hers wasn't so bad. Ham had appointed her co-investigative reporter, along with him. Besides being editor, he told her he wanted to write a story that would "blow the chimney off Kennedy Middle School." Though he had no idea of what that story might be, he was sure that between the two of them, they'd find it.

Gretchen had her doubts. The things that he had mentioned—the principal embezzling school funds, for instance—didn't seem likely possibilities.

Trying to come up with an exposé idea was tiring. Maybe I'll shut my eyes for a few seconds, she thought wearily, snuggling against her pillow. She was just drifting off when the phone rang. Gretchen wasn't even thinking about Tim as she fumbled for the receiver. So when she heard his voice, it was like a shock to her system.

"Gretchen? Is that you? It's Tim."

C H A P T E R
SEVEN

Gretchen put down the telephone with shaking hands. Then she steadied herself enough to dial Robin. "Can you come over right now? I need to see you. Tim just called."

The girls usually weren't allowed to visit each other on school nights, but Robin pleaded a forgotten assignment and the need to look at Gretchen's math book. Mrs. Miller was going to make a quick stop at the grocery store before picking Robin up, so the girls immediately sequestered themselves in Gretchen's den and talked fast.

"Then what did he say?" Robin asked, wide-eyed.

Gretchen thought back on the conversation, which was already all jumbled in her head.

"He said he was surprised when Bobby gave him my phone number. 'I never expected to hear from you.' I remember his saying that. He thought I was shy."

"What did you say?"

"I said I was. It was kind of awkward. There were some awfully long silences, but finally he said that he wasn't sure of his schedule, because of the shooting and all, but that he thought he could meet me at The Hut at four o'clock on Friday."

"Friday!" Robin sat up straight. "That's four days from now."

Gretchen wasn't sure if that made her happy or sad. On one hand, she wanted to get this date, or whatever it was, over. But she didn't know if she was ready to deal with Tim quite yet.

"It'll give you time anyway," Robin continued.

"Time for what?"

"To plan what you're going to wear, for one thing."

"Not more outfit planning," Gretchen groaned. "Golly, sometimes I think that's all I do."

"I'll bring my makeup." Robin was beginning to get into the plan.

This was getting complicated. "I thought you didn't want me to do this."

Robin shrugged. "I thought you weren't paying attention to me."

"Maybe we could just tell Veronica he called. She knows I don't actually have to go out with him. Technically, I've already won the bet."

"Like she'd believe you."

"No, I guess you're right. She wouldn't even believe it if both of us told her," Gretchen said, chewing on her lip.

The girls looked at each other silently for a few seconds.

"I'm still not totally sold on this idea," Robin said, "but you're only going to The Hut. It's not like anything could really happen. It *is* kind of neat, going out with a real actor."

"You'll have to make sure Veronica's at The Hut. So she can have her proof."

"That shouldn't be too difficult." Robin reached over for some of the popcorn Gretchen had made while waiting for her to arrive. "She'll want to be there to see it all."

"Well, at least Veronica will get put in her place for once."

Robin slowly chewed her popcorn.

"Gretchen, do you think Veronica's getting any better?"

"Better than what?"

"Than she used to be."

"Oh, yeah, she's a real sweetheart now," Gretchen said sarcastically.

Robin sighed. "I don't know what to do about her. I think she is trying to act a little nicer."

"Right. Now she just says a lot of mean things and pretends she's doing it for your own good."

"She's having a sleep-over," Robin said quietly. "She asked me and Sharon, and she said she's going to ask you, too."

"Me?" Gretchen asked, startled.

"Saturday night."

"I'm not going. I know what would happen. She'd just start making fun of me." Gretchen peered at Robin. "You don't want to go, do you?"

Robin looked uncomfortable. "We were best friends for so long. She doesn't seem as bad as she used to be. Maybe I should give her a chance."

The worried knot inside Gretchen's stomach pulled itself a tad tighter. Gretchen knew that sixth-grade friendships shifted like sands in the desert, but she had thought for sure that Robin was through with Veronica. Now it seemed she wasn't.

"Then you are going," Gretchen said carefully.

"Not if you don't want to. But I wish everybody could be friends."

Gretchen suddenly felt as old as Tim thought she was. Certainly old enough to know that Robin might as well wish for the tooth fairy to come or for Santa to personally place the presents under the tree.

"Think about it anyway, won't you?" Robin asked.

"Sure. I'll think about it." But silently she added, Don't count on it.

Mrs. Miller honked for Robin and the girls got up. As they walked into the hall, Robin whispered, "What are you going to tell your father about Tim?"

Gretchen looked at him sitting alone in the kitchen. "Nothing."

"What if he finds out?" Robin asked as she got her jacket from the closet.

"I'm just meeting this guy for a Coke. Then I'll never see him again."

"But what if he calls and your dad answers?"

Gretchen hadn't considered this horrible possibility. "I don't know." She was beginning to feel like a fly caught in a web of lies.

"Well, that probably won't happen," Robin said philosophically.

"I'll just say it's one of the boys from school, I guess." Add another delicate strand to the web.

After Robin left, Gretchen headed up to her room, but her father's voice stopped her. "Gretchen, can you come in here?"

Gretchen walked reluctantly into the kitchen.

"Sit down with me for a few minutes. It seems like we've been missing each other the last couple of days."

It was true. With all that was swirling around her lately, Gretchen hadn't seen her dad much. The truth of the matter was, she had been avoiding him. This whole thing with Tim was making her nervous, and her father was pretty good at telling when she was upset. Even better than her mom maybe.

"So how's school?" Mr. Hubbard asked.

"Fine."

"That's it?"

Gretchen slowly sat down. Why was it parents always wanted you to talk just when you least felt like it? You'd think they'd have

104

enough problems just trying to pay the bills and get the laundry done.

"It seems like you've had something on your mind." Her father peered at her.

Gretchen decided to get some answers for herself. Why should she always be the one to answer questions? "You don't seem very happy yourself."

At least she had startled him. Mr. Hubbard got up and started to clear a few remaining plates. "I'm doing okay."

"You don't do any of the things you used to. You used to go bowling."

"My back's been bothering me," her father murmured as he rinsed the dishes under the faucet.

Gretchen immediately felt bad. "Are you going to the doctor?"

"No, no, it's nothing serious. Don't worry about it. I just haven't felt like going out much."

"You need a vacation, Dad," Gretchen said automatically. Whenever he complained about working too hard that's what Mrs. Hubbard had told her husband. But he almost never took time off, so Gretchen was shocked when he replied, his back still to her, "Yes, I'm considering getting away for a few days."

"You are!"

"Uh-huh." Finally he turned and faced her. "What would you think about that?"

"Well, it would be great," she said slowly. "Where would you go?"

"I'm not sure yet."

"Would I come with you?"

Her father gave her a tired smile. "I don't think so. Would that upset you?"

"Not if I could stay with Robin."

"Actually I was thinking about having Mrs. Coppick come in."

Gretchen groaned. "Not Mrs. Coppick!"

Mrs. Coppick had been her baby-sitter for longer than she cared to remember, longer than she was able to remember actually. Somewhere in a photo album there was a picture of Mrs. Coppick sitting next to Gretchen while she was on the potty. She reminded herself to find that picture and tear it up.

It wasn't that Mrs. Coppick wasn't nice. She was too nice. When Gretchen was younger, she had enjoyed the way Mrs. Coppick was always ready to play dolls with her or color in a coloring book. But Mrs. Coppick didn't seem to realize that Gretchen was growing up. She still asked Gretchen if she wanted to play Candy Land.

For the last year, after a great deal of pleading on Gretchen's part, her parents had finally agreed to let her stay alone when they went out at night. She had been just fine. Oh, the first evening she had walked around the house a couple of times, looking in closets and picking up the phone just to make sure it was in working order in case she had to dial 911. But by the end of the night, she was reading her new mystery and didn't even hear her parents come in the door. Now that she had baby-sat herself a couple of times, she assumed she'd never have to see Mrs. Coppick again. She hoped the woman was spending her time with kids who might actually want to play Candy Land. Hearing Mrs. Coppick's name was like that advertisement for the fifth installment of a horror movie: "She-e-e's back!"

"Gretchen, I wouldn't think of imposing on the Millers for a couple of days," her dad informed her.

"They wouldn't mind," Gretchen whined.

"My plans aren't even definite yet. We'll see."

Her father's "we'll see"s were never that promising. She had a sinking feeling Mrs. Coppick was in her future. Just like Tim.

The next day Gretchen made sure she got to school early. She sat on the steps of the building, waiting for Veronica to appear. Finally the school bus pulled up and Veronica got off.

Candy was right behind her—no surprise there. Gretchen tried to look casual. She might as well tell both of them her good news at the same time.

"Hello," Gretchen said as they passed by on their way inside.

"Oh, hi." Veronica barely looked down at her.

"Just a minute. What are you two doing Friday after school?"

"Why?" Candy asked.

Gretchen didn't say anything. Now it was her turn to wear a mysterious smile, the same one that Veronica usually sported.

Veronica got it first. "Tim?"

"Tim," Gretchen replied, a lot more gaily than she really felt. "Our first date."

Gretchen had always supposed, if the occasion arose, she'd get plenty of satisfaction out of making some mean-spirited remarks to Veronica, the kind that really hurt. She had no idea that utter silence could be so satisfying. Finally, as she got up, she said, "Four o'clock. The Hut."

She walked inside without a backward glance.

But other than that memorable moment, Gretchen tried not to think about Tim. Fortunately most of her time was taken up with Ham and the class newspaper. Besides being co-investigative reporter, he had chosen her as his newspaper confidant. Ham needed one, because he was in a tizzy about what they should do as their exposé.

Every afternoon, Mrs. Volini devoted the last period of the day to the newspaper. Part of Ham's time was spent checking in with everyone, but he also used much of it to talk to Gretchen.

"This is driving me nuts," Ham said on Thursday, hands stuck in his pockets, as he leaned against the blackboard. "Why can't I come up with an idea that will blow this school away?"

"Because nothing ever happens here?" Gretchen suggested as she doodled on a piece of paper.

"But what about our readers' right to know?"

"That's the problem," Gretchen said, looking up. "Veronica probably had it figured. What kids need to know is the time the baseball game starts and when auditions are being held for the spring play."

"Traitor!" Ham hissed.

"Ham, we've been trying for three days

now to find a story to investigate. Doesn't it tell you something that we haven't come up with one idea?"

"Yeah, we're not thinking hard enough," Ham said stubbornly.

"Let's go over it again. We have enough supplies, our books are brand-new, nobody's trying to get any books banned. We checked with the librarian. The teachers have a new contract and aren't even complaining about money. I don't know what that leaves."

Ham snapped his fingers. "Food."

"You're hungry?"

"I'm always hungry, but that's not what I mean. Remember that little kid in the cafeteria, the one who thought something was crawling on her meat?"

Gretchen shuddered. "How can I forget?"

"I thought she was going to puke."

"Ham! Gross!"

"Sorry. But that food almost made her sick."

"It doesn't seem to bother you. You eat it almost every day."

"My mother says I'll eat anything that doesn't eat me first," Ham admitted. "That doesn't mean it's any good."

"But what exactly would we write about?"

"I'm not sure," Ham replied thoughtfully, "but I think there's a story there."

"Your nose for news?"

"This time it's a feeling in the pit of my stomach. Let's go down to the cafeteria. Maybe something will hit us."

"Now?" Gretchen asked with surprise.

"Why not?"

Telling Mrs. Volini they needed to check out a story, Ham and Gretchen got permission to leave the room. Gretchen followed Ham downstairs, asking him questions all the way. "What is so important about the cafeteria that we have to go there right this minute? What if someone asks us what we're doing?"

Finally, as they entered the cafeteria, Ham said, "I want to get a feel for it, Gretchen. I want to soak up the atmosphere before we figure out what we should write about."

Gretchen looked around in bewilderment. "There is no atmosphere. This doesn't even look like our cafeteria."

The room, devoid of people, its tables clean, seemed totally different from the way it did in the middle of a noisy noon. This did not seem to dismay Ham, who began rubbing his hands together excitedly. "This is where it's all going to happen for us, Gretchen."

She could see it now, a big empty space on the front page where their story was supposed to be.

Ham began pacing. "What do the kids at Kennedy think about the cafeteria food?"

"No big news flash there. They hate it."

"But why is it so bad? I mean, do the cooks stink, or is the stuff they buy cheap? And if it is cheap, why is it cheap? Isn't there enough money to feed us properly?"

Gretchen stared at Ham. He was a man possessed.

Ham whirled around and looked at Gretchen. "Wouldn't you want to know why everything tastes so bad?"

"It's good for my diet," Gretchen said with a shrug. "But you might have something there."

"Sure I do. Everybody's interested in food."

Maybe not as much as you, Gretchen thought. Still, this was beginning to sound as if it had potential. "You've asked some good questions, Ham. But where do we start getting answers?" Gretchen asked.

Ham's smile faded. "I'm . . . not sure."

They thought for a moment.

"Should we interview Mrs. Stewart?" Gretchen suggested. "She is the head cook, after all."

"Good idea. She may try to stonewall us, though."

"Stonewall?"

"Not talk to us. But don't worry, we'll worm the information out of her," Ham replied, confident once more.

Mrs. Stewart was a tall tough-looking woman in her sixties. She wore freshly starched aprons over short-sleeved dresses that exposed her sinewy arms. Behind her back, the kids called her Stewball, in honor of her Irish stew and dumplings, a watery brown liquid with lumps of meat and hard, golf ball–like dumplings. The meat was dark, the dumplings were white. That was the only way to tell them apart. While the cafeteria workers ladled out the food, Mrs. Stewart often stood off in a corner, her arms folded, watching the children move through the line. Her dour countenance did nothing to whet young appetites.

"She won't be easy to worm," Gretchen warned. "You'd better plan your questions carefully."

"What do you mean me? We're a team, remember, just like Woodward and Bernstein."

"Who are they?"

Ham shook his head. "Boy, you sure don't know your history. Woodward and Bernstein were reporters for the *Washington Post*. They dug around, got the whole story on the Watergate break-in, and found out that President

Nixon and some of his advisers were behind it. Nixon had to resign."

"When was all this?"

"In the early seventies."

"That was years before I was born," Gretchen said. She couldn't get too worked up about it.

"Anyway, I think we should both do that interview. I'll set it up."

"All right, but let's get out of here now." She was beginning to get nervous. "We don't want to see old Stewball before we have our questions ready."

As Gretchen pawed through her locker after the last bell, trying to find her library book that needed returning, she felt a tap on her shoulder. There stood Veronica, looking a little pouty.

"Gretchen, I asked you to my sleep-over two days ago. You haven't even bothered to tell me yet if you're coming."

That was because Gretchen had changed her mind a million times on the subject. She had certainly been surprised when Veronica asked her, especially after their encounter on the school steps. But she supposed it was because Veronica thought Robin might not go if Gretchen wasn't invited.

Gretchen's gut feeling was still that she wanted no part of being in her pajamas with Veronica, Candy, and the rest of the group. But if Robin decided to join them, Gretchen thought that she'd better be there, too, just to keep an eye on things. It wasn't a feeling that made her proud.

"Oh, I guess I'll come," she finally answered, trying to sound nonchalant.

"You don't sound very sure."

"Who knows what will come up?"

"Do whatever you want. You will be at The Hut tomorrow?"

"Of course." Gretchen slammed the locker door shut.

"It's the big day," Veronica said brightly.

"Yeah," Gretchen agreed as she sidestepped Veronica and headed toward the doors. But whoever said bigger was better had it all wrong. She should have known that from when she was fat.

CHAPTER
EIGHT

Ham looked down at Gretchen, who was sitting on one of the stone benches in front of the school. She didn't notice him until he poked her foot and said, "What's with you?"

Gretchen considered. Did she want to explain that in less than seven hours she'd be walking into The Hut, trying to pass as a high-school girl? She did not. "Nothing."

"Good. Because I don't want you distracted. It's all set up."

"What is?"

"The meeting with Mrs. Stewart. Accent on the stew, which is one of the dishes I'm going to ask her about. You've put together some questions, haven't you?"

Gretchen nodded.

"Good. We can go over them before we go down there."

"When is this meeting?" Gretchen asked dully.

"After school. Three-thirty."

That woke Gretchen up. "Three-thirty! No way! I have an appointment of my own at four."

"Dentist, doctor?"

"Never mind."

Ham shook his head. "If it's not something medical, forget it, Gretchen. Mrs. Stewart didn't want to see us at all. I'll never get another appointment."

"Then go yourself. I can give you my questions."

For the first time since he had assumed the job—and the commanding air—of editor-in-chief, Ham seemed totally lost. "I can't."

"Why can't you?"

"Mrs. Stewart gives me the willies. I had nightmares about her last night. Real nightmares, Gretchen. She was trying to stick me in a vat of spaghetti sauce."

Ham looked so stricken, Gretchen had to stifle a laugh. "I'm surprised the idea didn't appeal to you," she said, trying to keep a straight face.

"Don't tell anyone this," Ham continued,

"but I've gotta have someone with me. You."

"I told you. . . ."

"Please," Ham said humbly.

This was all she needed—Ham looking like a puppy dog, his eyes big and pleading. "All right," she said, relenting. "I can be there for fifteen minutes. That's all. Then I have to get to my appointment."

"Fifteen minutes," Ham said with relief. "Great!"

With a sigh, Gretchen watched Ham hurry off. She had wanted to get to The Hut early, to have time to collect herself. Well, she was stuck now. She saw Robin heading inside and waved her over. Quickly she filled her in on the change in plans.

"I don't see how you let Ham talk you into this," Robin said.

Gretchen didn't want to embarrass Ham. "Aw, it's for school. And I can still be there in time."

Robin looked Gretchen over. "You look great."

Gretchen had spent extra time getting her hair to look just right. She had borrowed a Northwestern University sweatshirt from Robin, hoping it might make Tim think she was a high schooler with college on her mind.

She had also worn her tightest-fitting leggings. "Thanks. Did you bring the makeup?"

"Yes, but you've got to allow a few extra minutes to put it on," Robin reminded her.

Gretchen clapped her hand against her forehead. "I forgot."

"Boy, this dating stuff is harder than it looks," Robin said as they walked into the school.

It was a strange day. Sometimes the moments passed interminably, seeming more like hours. But then at other times the day seemed to be going all too fast. At some point in the afternoon, Veronica passed her a note. All it said was, "I can't wait. What about you?" Gretchen made a face and shoved the paper in her purse.

As the last bell began ringing, Gretchen jumped up, grabbed her belongings, and almost ran over to Ham's desk. "I'll meet you in the cafeteria." Before he could say anything, she rushed over to Robin. "Let's get to the bathroom and put on the makeup."

Shoving their way through the halls, they made it to the girls' bathroom in record time. It was full of fourth- and fifth-grade girls waiting in line for a stall.

"Over here," Robin said. There was a corner near the window that was empty. "What have you got with you?"

Gretchen pulled out the lipstick and blusher. "I found some of my mother's old mascara, too."

"Great," Robin said. "Let's get to work."

With a trembling hand, Gretchen opened the blusher, looked in the mirror, and began stroking color on her cheeks. "I'm not putting on too much, am I?"

Robin looked at her critically. "Maybe on the left." She pulled out a tissue, and Gretchen dabbed frantically. "I don't have time for repair work."

"What are you doing?"

The girls looked down at a small fourth grader, who was observing them with interest.

"Putting on makeup. What does it look like?" Robin said as Gretchen began applying the lipstick.

"I didn't think makeup was allowed at Kennedy," the girl continued.

"It's not. School's over." Gretchen tried not to mess up the lipstick as she spoke.

"But you're still in the bathroom."

"Beat it," Gretchen said through tight lips.

"Boy, you must be nervous." Robin watched the girl scurry away. "You're always so nice to little kids."

"I used to be lots of things: honest, reliable . . . and fat. Boys didn't want to meet me at The Hut then."

"Well, it's better this way, isn't it?"

Gretchen wasn't sure. After a few licks with the mascara, she asked Robin, "How do I look?"

"Terrific," Robin replied.

Gretchen could tell Robin was telling the truth. "What time is it?"

"Almost three-thirty."

"I'd better get to the cafeteria."

Robin nodded. "I'll meet you at The Hut. Veronica and I will be sitting at the back."

"I'll try to ignore you."

By the time Gretchen got to the cafeteria, she was out of breath. She hoped that Ham would already be interviewing Mrs. Stewart, but he was just sitting in the empty lunchroom, his feet stretched out in front of him.

"Where is she?" Gretchen asked, practically yelling. "I thought you'd be in the middle of the interview by now."

Ham barely looked up. "I don't know. Having a conversation with some carrots maybe. I got here right on time, and she told me to wait."

"Ham, twelve minutes before I'm out of here," she said grimly.

"Gretchen . . ." He glanced at her, then stared. "Gretchen!"

"What?" she asked nervously.

"You look . . . fantas—great. You look really great!"

"Thanks."

Ham sprang to his feet and circled her. "Maybe Robin should put your picture in the style section."

"Ham, quit it."

Snapping his fingers, he said, "Hey, I just had a great idea. Got any pictures of yourself when you were fat? We could do one of those before-and-after things. 'Heavy to Heavenly'—how's that for a headline?"

Through clenched teeth, Gretchen said, "If you don't get Mrs. Stewart right now, I'm leaving."

That woke Ham from his editorial reverie. "Okay, I'll find her. But I'm not done with this idea yet."

While Ham went back to the kitchen, Gretchen checked her makeup. It was amazing. She really did look like she was fourteen, fifteen maybe. It made her feel weird. She hoped Mrs. Stewart wouldn't say anything. Could a cook report a student for wearing makeup?

"Here she is," Ham said, coming back into

the cafeteria with Mrs. Stewart a few paces behind him. "We can start now."

"I don't see what all the rush is about," Mrs. Stewart said, sitting down at a table. "I was phoning in a meat order." She barely glanced at Gretchen.

"I have to leave in a few minutes," Gretchen said politely. "An appointment."

"All right," Mrs. Stewart replied huffily. "Just start asking your questions then."

Ham and Gretchen had written down their questions during last period. Gretchen looked over at Ham, expecting him to begin, but he was rummaging through his book bag, trying to find his notes. As disorganized as ever, Gretchen thought with a sigh. "Where do you get your ideas for your menus?" Gretchen finally asked.

"Get them? Why, the whole district has the same menus. Of course, I do add the occasional special dish, like my Irish stew." She looked proud.

Ham was still looking, so Gretchen continued. "Do all the schools have the same recipes?"

"No. If it's meat loaf, for instance, you are allowed some variation in the way it's prepared. My brother is a wholesale butcher, and he gives me tips about ways to prepare meat."

At this, Ham's head came up like a dog sniffing steak. "Did you say your brother?"

Mrs. Stewart gave him the fish-eye. "Yes, my brother. What of it?"

"Oh, nothing."

"Would you say the kids at Kennedy generally enjoy the food?" Gretchen asked cautiously.

"Wouldn't you?" Mrs. Stewart snapped.

"Say," Ham asked, "could we have a tour of the kitchen?"

Mrs. Stewart frowned. "Whatever for?"

Gretchen stared at Ham. This wasn't part of the plan.

"Oh," he answered vaguely, "we'd just like to see where it all happens."

Grudgingly Mrs. Stewart agreed. She led them out to the kitchen, where two industrial-size stoves and several dishwashers took up most of the room.

Ham ran his finger along the counter, a move not missed by Mrs. Stewart. "I keep this kitchen gleaming," she said, glaring at them.

"Oh, we can see that," Gretchen said hurriedly.

"Maybe we could print one of your recipes in the paper," Ham said, "as kind of a highlight. What about your recipe for Irish stew?"

"That's a family secret."

Ham and Gretchen exchanged looks. That figured.

Gretchen glanced at the cafeteria clock. "I'm sorry, but I have to go. Ham, you can handle the rest of this, right?"

Ham seemed to be his confident self once more. "Certainly, Gretchen," he said formally. "Good-bye, Bernstein."

"I thought her name was Hubbard," Mrs. Stewart remarked suspiciously.

Gretchen left Ham to answer that. Had they gotten anything from Mrs. Stewart worth writing about? Oh, well, it was time to slip out of her girl-reporter mode and become a femme fatale. Good-bye, Bernstein; hello, Julia Roberts.

She didn't know if she should run to The Hut or just walk at her usual pace. One way she'd be sweaty, the other way she'd be late. She decided to combine the two. When she felt little beads of sweat on her forehead, she slowed down.

It was exactly four when she arrived. Gretchen stood across the street for a minute, trying to see if Tim was inside. Yes, there he was, sitting near the window.

She couldn't help thinking that only a few months ago, as a very mean practical joke, Veronica had lured her to The Hut on the pretext that one of the cute boys in Mr. Jacobs's class liked her. Now a real movie actor was waiting for her. The nervousness slipped away and she just felt proud. How perfect that Veronica was having to watch it all.

The Hut wasn't terribly crowded, but the sixth-grade girls were there in full force. Out of the corner of her eye, she saw Robin, Veronica, Candy, Kim, Jessica, and Sharon squeezed in a back booth.

Tim might be the actor, but Gretchen suddenly felt as if she were the one in the movie. She was playing the role of a sophisticated young woman, used to having good-looking guys waiting for her. When she thought about it that way, she noted, she could really get into it.

Throwing back her shoulders a little, Gretchen glanced in Veronica's direction and then strolled over to Tim's table. "Hello." She smiled down at him.

Tim seemed genuinely glad to see her. "Hi, Gretchen, I was afraid you wouldn't come."

"You were?" she asked as she sat down. "Why?"

"I don't know. I haven't had much luck meeting girls since I've been here."

She couldn't seem to keep her eyes off those cute freckles. "But you must know a lot of girls on the set."

Tim shrugged. "They're all older."

And I'm younger, Gretchen thought, but luckily Tim didn't seem to notice.

"How did you get into movies in the first place?" This was one of the questions she had rehearsed. When she had been writing down questions for Mrs. Stewart, she had jotted down a few for Tim, too.

"It was all my mother's idea. She signed me up at a talent agency when I was just a baby."

"Were you talented then?"

Gretchen hadn't meant that as a joke, but apparently Tim thought she did. "Oh, yeah. I spit up better than any kid on the block." He smiled at her. "You're funny."

Gretchen tried to hide her confusion behind a smile. "So you were in commercials?"

"Yeah, mostly, and television shows. Small parts."

"Have I seen you in anything?"

Screwing up his face, Tim said in a high-pitched voice, "Mom, I like Beantown's beans best. They're the beaniest."

"You're the Beantown boy! But he's only . . ."

"I made it ten years ago, when I was five."

He's fifteen, Gretchen thought, her heart sinking. But all she said was, "I didn't know they showed commercials for that long."

"Usually they don't. But there are a couple of us, me and Mikey, that cereal kid, and the boy who spells out bologna, we keep getting hauled out year after year."

There was something about looking at Tim as the little Beantown boy that made him easier to talk to. Of course, he did most of the talking, telling Gretchen about *The Pocket Pickers*, how the tutor on the set functioned as the kids' chaperon, what Greg Marsh was like, and how different the Midwest was from L.A.

Maybe I do have a knack for being a reporter, Gretchen thought. All she had to do was ask a simple question like "Who picks out your costumes?" and Tim was off and running. Gretchen sat back and sipped at the Coke she'd ordered, every once in a while glancing over at Veronica, who was trying not to look glum.

Finally Tim said, "Hey, I've been monopolizing the conversation. You must think I'm just some Hollywood jerk."

"No, I don't." She was beginning to think he was pretty wonderful actually.

"Well, tell me something about you. I've

never gone to a regular high school. What's it like?"

"The high school is over on the other side of town." At least she knew that much, although the school's location was probably not the kind of fascinating detail Tim had in mind.

He laughed again, as if she had made another amusing remark. "That's the best you can say about it, huh?" He looked around. "Is that why there are hardly ever any older kids here? This place looks like Kiddieland, frankly."

"Most of the high-school kids do hang out at Willie's. It's closer to school."

"Then why don't you?"

Gretchen was saved by a ruckus in the corner. Two boys from the junior high started a pushing match, and the owner came over to break it up. "I—I have to go, Tim," Gretchen said, getting to her feet.

"Already?"

"I have to . . . baby-sit," she lied.

"Let me walk you there." Tim stood up, too.

"No, don't," Gretchen said, a little panicky. "I'm not allowed to have boys over," she improvised.

Tim shrugged. "Okay, I should be getting back to the motel anyway. We've got a late call this evening."

Gretchen felt extremely awkward. How did one end a date, if that's what this was?

"I'll call you sometime," Tim said. "My schedule's hectic."

"Sure, great," Gretchen said. "Bye." She pushed her way through the old screen door and took a gulp of air once she was outside. Her first date. Was she glad it was over, or did she wish it could have gone on forever? Gretchen wasn't sure.

She knew if she stood there for even another moment, the girls would appear. She didn't want to see them. She didn't want to do anything but get back to her bedroom, shut the door, and think about the last forty-five minutes. Glancing into The Hut, she could see Robin and the others standing up. Before they could get to the door, she started moving quickly down the street, faster and faster, until she was practically running in the direction of her house.

CHAPTER

NINE

"Hey, sleepyhead," her father greeted Gretchen the next morning. "I thought you weren't getting up at all."

"You were almost right," she answered as she headed to the refrigerator to pour herself some juice. Luxuriating in bed, rolling over and dreaming more about Tim, that was the way to while away the day.

"What are your plans?" Mr. Hubbard asked, folding up his newspaper.

Back to reality. "I have to meet Ham at the library. We're going to talk about our newspaper project." She paused. "I was invited to a sleep-over tonight."

"At Robin's?"

"No," Gretchen said quietly. "Veronica's."

"Veronica Volner? You're not thinking of going are you?" Confusion painted her dad's face. He was well aware of all the problems Veronica had caused for Gretchen.

Gretchen didn't know how to explain. She had talked to Robin only briefly yesterday evening. "Tell me, tell me," Robin had squealed. "Why did you leave? We all wanted to hear."

Gretchen stiffened. "I didn't want to talk about it with everyone. Are you alone now?" she asked suspiciously.

Robin paused. "No, Veronica walked me home, and she hung around until my mother asked her to stay for supper."

Oh, great, thought Gretchen. She could feel herself getting angry at Robin. "Where is she?"

"Downstairs. Don't be mad."

"All right." Gretchen sighed. "But I'll talk to you tomorrow. Alone."

Robin got her point. "Okay. Call me."

After that, Gretchen had thought it might be better if she went to the stupid sleep-over. She didn't want to make Robin stay home or, worse, have her go alone. Then Veronica could really get her hooks into Robin. "I haven't been to a sleep-over in a while," Gretchen told her father. "It might be fun," she said carefully.

"Well, don't let that girl intimidate you," her father said forcefully. "You have more on the ball than she ever will." Mr. Hubbard's voice softened. "Do you know what a wonderful kid you are, Gretchen?"

Gretchen shook her head in embarrassment.

"It's true. Why, I expect to be tripping over boys one day."

Gretchen didn't want to hear that. "I'd better get to the library." She put her juice glass in the sink and turned to go. Her father's voice stopped her.

"I have to talk to you about something."

"What?"

"I'm going to Santa Fe next weekend."

"You are!" Gretchen practically clapped her hands.

"I don't know what's going to happen," Mr. Hubbard warned. "Your mother and I just want to talk face-to-face."

"Oh, Daddy, tell her to come home," Gretchen pleaded.

"I know that's what you want, but, honey, please don't get your hopes up."

"You mean you might . . . ?"

"I mean don't jump to conclusions one way or the other." Mr. Hubbard ran a hand through his hair. "I just don't know what's going to happen."

She forced herself to ask the question she had been afraid to utter for months. "But you and Mom still love each other, don't you?"

"Gretchen . . . ," Mr. Hubbard began, embarrassed.

"Daddy, I need to know." All her scared feelings, the ones she had been trying so hard to push down inside her, came bubbling to the surface.

Mr. Hubbard seemed to realize this. "I still love her. I've been mad that she felt she had to go away, but it was a wonderful opportunity for her. It wasn't doing any of us any good for her to be so unhappy. But now I wish she'd come home."

There was a look on her father's face that Gretchen couldn't quite place. Then she recognized it. He was scared. She went over to him and gave him a hug, feeling like he was the child instead of her. "It'll be okay," she whispered.

"Sure it will," he said shyly. "There's one other thing I have to tell you about next weekend, though."

Gretchen pulled back and looked at him. "Not Mrs. Coppick."

"Mrs. Coppick. I won't feel comfortable any other way, Gretchen."

"But we haven't even asked the Millers!"

"Because I don't want to impose."

"But . . ."

"Gretchen, please."

Gretchen could see that she was only irritating her father. "All right, Mrs. Coppick."

"Thank you," her father said, relieved. "Now, do you want me to drive you over to the library?"

"No, it's a nice day. I'll walk." She could use the exercise. First, though, she went into the television room and dialed Robin's number. "Hi. Are you finally alone?" She couldn't help sounding just a little sarcastic.

"Yes."

"Did Veronica sleep over last night?"

"No."

"But you're going to her sleep-over tonight." It was a statement not a question.

"I told you I don't have to. But it might be fun, Gretchen. Gosh, this is your chance to lord it over all of them. Veronica was practically green with jealousy."

Gretchen hadn't thought about it like that. She was sure the girls would find some way to make fun of her, but after all, she was the one having the last laugh. "I'm going," she finally said.

"If Veronica says one nasty thing, we'll leave," Robin promised.

"All right, I'll give it a shot."

Robin sounded more comfortable. "That's good. I just hate it when people are fighting. So tell me. I've been dying to hear what happened."

Gretchen settled in comfortably on the couch. "He was so cute," she began. She spent the next hour going over every detail of her "date." She and Robin spent more time talking about Tim than she and Tim had actually spent at The Hut. Glancing over at the clock she let out a small shriek. "I'm late for the library, Robin. Ham is going to kill me. We're supposed to go over the cafeteria story."

"He can't kill you. He needs you too much."

Gretchen thought Robin was probably right. "What are you doing this afternoon?"

"Going shopping with my mom. It's my dad's birthday."

Gretchen hadn't told Robin her other big news. "My dad's going to Santa Fe."

"To get back with your mom," Robin squealed.

"Keep your fingers crossed."

Gretchen decided she didn't have time to walk to the library after all. Her father dropped her off, and she found Ham in a corner of the reading room leafing through a magazine.

"What are you reading?" she asked, plopping down beside him on the couch.

Ham held up *Bon Appétit*. "You know, there are a lot of good recipes in this world."

"Too bad Mrs. Stewart doesn't know any. What happened after I left?"

Ham threw the magazine aside. "I think I've got it all figured out," he said, his voice quivering with excitement.

"You've figured out what?"

"Why the food is so bad," Ham said impatiently. "What do you think we're exposing?"

Gretchen folded her arms over her chest. "Okay, lay it on me."

"Stewball is using dog meat in the food!"

Gretchen started to laugh. "Oh, Ham, don't be silly."

"I'm not! Gretchen, just before I was ready to leave the cafeteria, I went back to the kitchen. There were two giant boxes in the corner labeled 'Woofers Dog Food.' The boxes even had a picture of a dog licking his chops."

"But was there dog food inside?"

"Well, I couldn't check it out. Stewball was standing right there." Ham was leaning toward Gretchen, practically in her face. Ham had freckles, too, she noticed, but they weren't having the same effect on her as Tim's.

"You have got a long way to go with this

story before we can print it," Gretchen said. "This is nothing."

"It's a start," Ham replied, obviously disappointed in her lackluster response.

Gretchen considered this. "It's just an idea, Ham, not a start."

"Okay, so we'll get proof."

"How?"

"I'll figure it out," Ham said irritably.

"You still have to organize the rest of the paper. And you and Bobby have to finish that story about moviemaking in Forest Glen. Are you sure you're going to have time for this big exposé?"

"We have all of next week to get copy in and then another week to lay out the paper before it gets printed. But this is at the top of the list. It's the kind of story that gets a reporter's blood flowing."

Gretchen made a face. Who wanted to think of Ham's blood racing around his body? "I suppose the first thing we'd better do is go back to the cafeteria and see if there really is dog food in those cartons."

"Right," Ham said approvingly. "Check it out on Monday."

"Me!"

"You just said I'm going to be busy."

"But what if somebody tries to stop me?"

"Hey, do you think anyone could have stopped Bernstein?"

"I'm getting real tired of hearing about Bernstein."

"Gretchen, you've got to investigate. It's for your fellow students." Ham looked at her earnestly.

"They never did much for me," Gretchen muttered. Finally she said, "I'll try, Ham. But this is a dopey idea."

Ham smiled. "We'll see."

As she packed her duffel bag that evening, it occurred to Gretchen that checking out cartons of dog food might seem like a lot of fun compared to this sleep-over. She stuffed some clothes for the next day into her bag, then wondered what kind of sleepwear she should take. It was too warm for her favorite flannel pajamas, which also would have done the best job of covering her up. Without a bra, Gretchen's chest looked even bigger, and she was afraid the other girls would tease her.

Gretchen paused and looked at herself in the mirror. Standing up straight, for once, she could see just how developed she was. She knew that lots of girls wished for just what she had, but Gretchen didn't feel ready for it yet. She wasn't used to it either. You don't notice getting taller or your arms getting longer, but you certainly noticed this. Gretchen was sure other people did, too.

She walked over to her pajama drawer. When her mother had been home, she always washed and neatly folded Gretchen's clothes before putting them in the drawer. Gretchen's style was to stuff them in. As she discarded a sleepshirt with babyish snowmen all over it and a nightgown with a hole in it, Gretchen looked in another drawer and found one of her father's old college T-shirts. It was large and stretched out, and it looked kind of cool. She decided it would make a statement and was no more revealing than any of the rest of her sleepwear.

Longingly, she looked at her stuffed monkey, Cleo, hanging crazily from her headboard. Cleo had gotten her through some pretty hard times, and she would have loved to have her along on this caper. "Sorry, Cleo," Gretchen whispered. "Veronica would have a real laugh over you."

After she finished her packing, Gretchen flopped on her bed and closed her eyes. She knew she should get up and do some homework, or even read her current mystery, but just lying there seemed a lot easier.

Why did life have to be so complicated? When she had been fat and virtually friendless, she had been miserable. Oh, she hid it

140

from her parents, and even herself, sometimes. She did her homework, got high grades, and was a good, obedient child. Heck, she never had a chance to be much else. But she had longed to be a part of a group, to whisper and giggle and know secrets. Well, tonight she might be, but that wasn't making her very happy either. She couldn't remember the last time she had been to a group sleep-over. As far as knowing how to act, she might as well be going to tea with the queen of England.

Gretchen followed Robin down the stairs to Veronica's rec room. Over Robin's shoulder, she could see Veronica at the tape deck, changing tapes. Kim and Natalie were giggling on the couch. They looked up as she and Robin clattered down the stairs. Were they talking about her? Gretchen wondered. At least Sharon, sitting on the floor with Jessica, gave her a friendly wave.

Veronica glanced up from her tapes. "Hi, Robin."

Slighted already, Gretchen thought.

But then Veronica turned to Gretchen. "I guess you decided to come." Her tone was flat, no inflection at all.

"Here I am." Gretchen's voice matched Veronica's.

"So what's this surprise you have for us?" Kim interrupted.

"Surprise?" Robin asked sharply.

"Not yet," Veronica replied. "Later."

Gretchen looked at Robin. Her expression clearly said, This had better not be about me.

"Where's Candy?" Robin asked.

"She'll be here soon."

"Do you think we should wait until she gets here for the big presentation?" Without anyone else seeing, Robin nudged Gretchen's foot.

"What are you talking about?" Veronica asked with a frown.

"Gretchen won her bet. You have to give her your Harvard sweatshirt." Robin smiled sweetly.

"Oh, that," Veronica said with a dismissive wave of her hand. "She can get it when she leaves tomorrow."

The other girls drew closer as Gretchen cleared her throat and said, "I'd like you to give it to me now. After all, I did win."

"Oh, all right," Veronica said. As she stomped upstairs, Gretchen realized that this evening might not be so bad after all.

With Veronica gone, the other girls were excited to hear about Gretchen's date. "So what was it like?" Kim wanted to know.

"I hear he was the Beantown boy," Natalie chimed in.

Gretchen settled down on the couch to tell her story, which sounded wonderful even to her own ears. At one point, Candy came into the room, stood behind the couch, and listened wistfully. Gretchen knew just how she felt.

Veronica did not make it downstairs through the whole telling. But perhaps she was just standing on the stairs, waiting for Gretchen to finish. She finally came back down as Sharon was saying, with a sigh, "You're so lucky," and threw the sweatshirt over to Gretchen. "It's yours."

"Thank you," Gretchen said. "I guess I did win it fair and square." It was a sweet moment.

Veronica scowled and brought out her new Ouija board, informing the girls that this was a mystical way to tell the future. It was the surprise, and her way of directing the attention from Gretchen.

"Here's how it works. Two of us put our hands on the pointer. We don't move it," she emphasized, "it moves itself. It answers questions by pointing out the letters on the board. Robin and I will start."

Robin shook her head. "Do it with someone else."

Veronica looked disappointed, but she said, "All right, Natalie, let's set up some chairs. We put the board on our knees."

When the girls were ready, Robin started off with a question. "Who am I going to marry?"

The pointer moved to the letter *J* then *O*. "Jon," the girls shrieked. Gretchen was sure that Veronica had pushed the pointer.

Kim asked where she was going to college, and Jessica wanted to know what she was going to be when she grew up.

"Don't you want to ask anything, Gretchen?" Robin wanted to know.

"Not me. I've had enough excitement for a while."

When the girls had finally finished with the Ouija board and had eaten the pizza Veronica ordered, they decided to play Truth or Dare. Each girl was allowed to ask someone else a question. If the respondent didn't tell the truth, she had to take the group's dare.

"I'll start," Veronica said. "Gretchen."

Gretchen could feel herself tighten up.

"How big is your bust?"

Candy and Kim giggled.

Gretchen didn't want to answer, but she knew that if she didn't, Veronica had some awful dare in mind. "Thirty-four-B."

"B," Kim whispered. "Wow."

That led off a round of truths about everyone's bra size. Jessica, who was a tiny little thing, refused to answer. "I don't know, I tell you."

"Well, what size undershirt do you wear?" Natalie asked with a laugh.

"If Jessica won't answer or can't," Veronica said over Jessica's protests, "we have to give her a dare."

The girls thought about it for a few minutes, while Jessica still tried to make a case for not deserving one.

"I know," Candy said. "Let's have her call Greg Marsh."

"I can't do that," Jessica said as the other girls laughed and said, "Yes, yes."

"I don't even know where he's staying."

"The Ramada Inn on Route Forty-one," Kim said smugly. "Bobby told me that's where all the movie people are staying."

"I'll get the number," Candy said. She jumped up and dialed information. "Here it is," she said, shoving the cordless phone and the number at Jessica.

"What am I supposed to say to him?" Jessica wailed.

"That's up to you," Veronica said.

Now Jessica started to laugh along with everyone else. "All right, I know what I'm going to say." Quickly she began dialing the motel.

Jessica's voice was usually high, but she lowered it to a husky purr as she told the motel operator, "Please put me through to Mr. Marsh."

The other girls hid their giggles behind their hands. Robin had to stuff a napkin in her mouth.

"Oh, but I'm sure he'd like to talk to me." There was a pause. "Oh, okay. Well, would you tell him Candy Dahl called? My number is . . ." As she gave the Dahl's phone number, Candy began hitting her. "Tell him I love him and . . ." Before she could say any more, Candy pushed down the button on the phone.

"Hey, that wasn't funny," Candy said, but she was drowned out by gales of laughter.

It took the girls a while to calm down.

"Candy, what if he calls?" Robin said.

"Yeah, right."

"Then you and Gretchen could both be dating movie stars."

It was an offhand comment from Kim, but Gretchen felt pleased nevertheless. After all, she really had had a date with an actor.

The game resumed. Natalie wanted to know how far Robin had gone with Jonathan. Embarrassed, she replied, "Just a kiss."

Then it was Gretchen's turn. She looked

around the circle. Feeling powerful, she zeroed in on Veronica. "Veronica, truth or dare, who in this room do you want to be your best friend?"

Candy looked expectant. But it was plain that Veronica's eyes had darted toward Robin. Robin noticed it, too, and turned her head away.

"Candy," Veronica finally said unconvincingly.

The game continued, but Gretchen didn't pay too much attention. Now Robin could see what Veronica was up to. From every angle, this evening was turning out to be a huge success.

CHAPTER
TEN

It was one of those days that felt more like summer than spring. Gretchen decided that a bike ride was what she needed to clear her head. Biking was great that way. You could think really hard about something and almost be unaware that you were peddling down the street. Or you could concentrate on the biking, without a thought in your head.

Gretchen was hoping that she could do the latter, but her mother's most recent phone call wouldn't go away. Earlier in the morning, Gretchen had come home from the sleep-over, ready to nap for a few hours while her father was out doing errands. Before she could get settled, the phone rang.

"How are you?" Mrs. Hubbard asked. "I haven't gotten a letter from you in a week."

"I've been busy."

"Doing what?"

Oh, dating a boy, Gretchen thought to herself, making Veronica Volner jealous. But all she said was, "I've had lots of homework. And that newspaper project I wrote you about."

"Yes, it sounded like fun. Another writer in the family."

Gretchen decided to get the direction of the conversation off her and on to more important matters. "Mom, Dad's coming down this weekend." Then she felt foolish. Of course her mother knew that.

"I want you to be good for Mrs. Coppick."

"I'm not going to hide her glasses, if that's what you mean." Gretchen had done that once, when she was about seven.

"You could make a lot more trouble for her now," Mrs. Hubbard said dryly.

"I still think I should have stayed with Robin. It's just three days."

"Gretchen, it's all arranged."

Gretchen suddenly woke up to what her mother was doing. Just as Gretchen had changed the subject, Mrs. Hubbard didn't want to talk about the upcoming weekend.

"Are you excited about Dad's visit?" she asked pointedly.

There was a hesitation. "Nervous is more like it."

"Dad's real excited about it."

"Is he?"

Gretchen couldn't tell if that was hope she heard in her mother's voice or apprehension. "Mom, have you decided what you're going to do? About coming back this summer, I mean."

Now Mrs. Hubbard put on the no-nonsense tone Gretchen was used to. "It will all get worked out. I don't want you to worry about it."

As Gretchen peddled along, she thought about what a silly statement that was. *Don't worry. After all, it's only your life we're talking about here. Let us grown-ups worry about it. We never make mistakes.* Oh, right, absolutely right.

She rode a little faster, trying to think of how she could make the situation with her parents turn out the way she wanted it to. She was riding so fast that she almost ran into Bobby Glickman, out walking his dog.

"Hey," he said, jumping out of the way. His black Lab just barked at her.

"Oh, sorry," Gretchen said, embarrassed.

"Where were you? Outer space?"

Gretchen could feel herself flushing. Bobby probably thought she was thinking about Tim, when it was her parents who were on her mind, for goodness' sake. She hoped that Bobby wouldn't ask her about Tim, but the next words out of his mouth were, "I heard you and Tim had a pretty good time."

Gretchen forgot that she didn't want to talk about that subject. "You did? Tim told you that?"

Bobby shrugged. "He said you were nice. I suppose that meant he had fun."

"What else did he say?" Gretchen demanded.

"That's all."

"Just that I was nice?"

Now it was Bobby's turn to look embarrassed. "Hey, we don't sit around talking about girls. And if we did, the girls he should be talking about would be high schoolers," he added significantly.

They walked along, Gretchen pushing her bike. "It was just a dare," Gretchen said quietly. "I probably won't see him again. He's nice, though."

"Yeah, everyone on the set likes him."

"So how's the moviemaking going?"

Bobby threw a stick for his dog to chase. "It's okay. Kind of boring actually."

"Yeah, it looked kind of dull that day we watched the shoot in the park."

"Here, Jacko." Bobby's dog raced over and dropped the stick at his feet. "Try telling that to most people. They think being in a movie is the most exciting thing in the world."

"Well, the idea of it is."

"Fantasy versus reality," he snorted.

Gretchen knew about that. But in some ways, reality was better than fantasy. She thought about how the girls' faces had looked at the sleep-over as she had regaled the group with details of her meeting with Tim. She hoped she'd have a lot of real moments like that.

School had taken on a new texture since the newspaper project began. There was a feeling in class like something was coming, like a turn in the weather. All day it seemed as if Mrs. Volini's class was just waiting for last period, when she dispersed the students to let them work on the newspaper. Ham had decided to call it the *Voice* because, he had told the class seriously, their paper would be the voice of truth.

Oddly, Ham's plan to have people report on things that normally wouldn't have interested them seemed to be working. Veronica's dislike of covering sports changed when Bobby, the movie star, offered to help her out. And Jonathan and Jason had taken to gossip with a real vigor. They had decided to call their column "Boys' Life," and from what Gretchen had heard, it was full of juicy nuggets, like which baseball player thought he was better than the rest of the guys on the team, and even who had a crush on whom—no names mentioned.

Reporters, editors, cartoonists, and even the kids who had to go to the other classrooms and collect money were up and excited about the project.

Ham continued to oversee everything, becoming even more enthusiastic than before, if possible. His zeal was going to rub off on that Woofers story, Gretchen was sure of that.

"Ham, I'm not going to that cafeteria alone," Gretchen told him decisively on Monday during the newspaper meeting.

Ham looked over his shoulder. Then he pulled a piece of paper out of his desk. It was dirty and crumpled, the way his homework always used to be. "Here, read this," he said, shoving it at Gretchen.

The more Gretchen read, the wider her eyes got. "Where did you get this stuff, Ham? It practically says the mystery meat is Woofers Dog Food. We don't know that yet."

Ham took the paper back. "Not yet. I just wrote this to see how it would sound."

"So you're not going to print it," Gretchen said, relieved.

"Not yet," Ham emphasized. "But once you check out those cartons . . ."

"We!" Gretchen's voice was so loud, several people turned around.

"Shh. Let's not let everyone in on it."

"We," she hissed.

"All right, we'll both go. Meet me in the hall as soon as the bell rings."

Feeling as though they were spies, which they were, really, Gretchen and Ham made their way into the empty cafeteria, and sneaked into the kitchen area.

"Good, there's nobody here," Ham whispered.

"Then why are you whispering?"

Ham didn't answer. Instead, he moved stealthily toward the corner behind the sink, where he had first seen the cartons of Woofers. He looked around. "They're gone," he said, disappointed.

Gretchen wasn't disappointed. She was absolutely relieved, until Ham snapped his fingers and said, "I get it. The meat loaf."

"What?"

"The meat loaf we had today," Ham said impatiently. "Don't you see? She must have used the dog food in that."

Gretchen hadn't eaten the meat loaf, but come to think of it, it had looked particularly awful, brown and crusty and covered with a tan goop. Could Ham possibly be right?

Ham lifted his head. "I think someone's coming."

"What should we do?" Gretchen asked desperately.

The footsteps were definitely coming from the direction of the cafeteria. They couldn't go back that way.

Now Ham looked a little panicky. "Let's go in there."

They ducked through a door into a dark, smelly corridor.

"Yuck," Gretchen said. "Where are we?"

"They must keep the garbage out here."

Gretchen glanced around. Sure enough, there were several large drums filled with garbage. "Let's go. Maybe that door over there leads to the outside."

Ham nodded, holding his nose. As he headed toward the door, he tripped over something, making a loud clattering noise. "What the . . . ?" He grabbed Gretchen's arm excitedly. "Look!" He picked up a couple of empty cans of Woofers Dog Food and practically shoved them at Gretchen.

"Oh, my gosh!" Her eyes grew wide.

The door from the kitchen was opening. Together they raced toward the exit that would lead them outside.

They kept running until they were at the edge of the school yard.

Huffing, Ham leaned against a tree, still clutching the cans. "Evidence," he gasped.

Gretchen grabbed at the can. "Oh, my gosh, oh, my gosh," she kept saying over and over.

"Well, this clinches it," Ham said.

"Wait a minute, we can't prove anything."

"This is going to be the biggest exposé ever." Ham stared off into space.

Gretchen could tell Ham was already at his computer, pounding out his lead story. "We need more proof," she insisted. "Woodman and Bernstein wouldn't have printed this story on the basis of a few empty cans."

"Woodward. Anyway, how can we get more info short of testing the meat?"

"We could ask Mrs. Stewart."

Ham looked at her incredulously. "Right, like she'd tell us the truth? She's probably pocketing the money she saves by not using the real stuff."

"Ham, think about it. This paper is part of learning about freedom of the press. We're going to look pretty stupid if we print a story that isn't true. I say we go back to the cafeteria and see if Mrs. Stewart is around and talk to her."

Ham wrinkled his nose.

"We have to try."

"Okay," he finally replied with a sigh. "But I still don't see how we can get her to admit anything."

"What should we do with those?" Gretchen pointed to the cans. "If we're right, we don't want her to see them."

Ham thought about that for a minute. "Let's bury them." He sank down to his knees and started to dig a hole. "Want to help me?"

Gretchen looked at Ham's dirty hands. "No."

Ham placed the cans carefully in the ground and covered the hole with a big rock to mark the spot. Gretchen said, "I guess we should find Mrs. Stewart now." But neither of them moved. "We've got to, Ham."

Slowly they trudged back to the cafeteria. Gretchen was half hoping Mrs. Stewart had gone for the day, but there she was, sitting in her office, doing paperwork. She looked up with a frown. "You two again?"

"We're still working on our story," Gretchen began tentatively.

"All right, have a seat. Now what do you want to ask me?"

Ham and Gretchen looked at each other. Where to begin? Ask if Woofers has all the nutritional value of a steak?

Gretchen cleared her throat. "The food you serve here, is it all ordered from one central source?"

"Of course. The district takes care of that."

"You can't get anything on your own?" Ham asked suspiciously.

"A few items. But just if we run out of ingredients."

Gretchen had an idea. "Do you get your own food from the district?"

"What do you mean?"

"You know, as kind of a perk. At a discount, maybe?"

Mrs. Stewart bristled. "Absolutely not. Why, all the food distributor has ever done for me is deliver some of my own groceries in bulk to the school."

"Oh, that's nice of him," Gretchen said, trying to appease her.

"Yes, well, it is helpful to have the dog food delivered here."

"Dog food?" Ham asked, with a gulp.

"Yes." Mrs. Stewart's face softened into a look approximating a smile. "I'm a volunteer at the Creatures-Be-Safe animal shelter. I donate a large percentage of the shelter's dog food. The school is closer to the shelter than my home, and a couple of the workers here help me load the dog food into my car. So I buy it through the district and have it delivered here."

"That's very nice of you," Gretchen said.

"What about the cans?" Ham asked.

"The cans?" Mrs. Stewart's face went back to its normal frown. "You mean how I recycle them?"

"Yes."

"Well, there's no recycling pickup at the shelter, so I bring them back here. But how in the world did you know about the cans?"

Ham jumped up. "The dentist."

"What?" Mrs. Stewart looked confused. "The dentist told you?"

"No, no. An appointment. Got to go." He pulled Gretchen by the arm. "We both have appointments."

"What exactly are you two going to write about the cafeteria anyway?" Mrs. Stewart was beginning to sound alarmed.

"Just the truth," Ham said with a sheepish grin. "Bye."

They didn't say a word until they left the building, well out of Mrs. Stewart's hearing. Then Gretchen muttered, "No, you didn't want to interview her, you just wanted to run with the story."

"I guess you're not the kind of person who minds saying, 'I told you so.'"

"Nope."

Ham kicked at the grass. "All right, all right, I was wrong. But what am I going to do now? This story was supposed to be the centerpiece of the newspaper. Now I've got a bunch of gossip, an article about how boring moviemaking is, a couple of cartoon strips, and a story about our terrible baseball team. Some newspaper. Some freedom of the press."

"Oh, Ham, think about it. Freedom of the press doesn't just mean writing down any crazy idea that comes into your head. The story has to be real."

"I thought it was real," Ham said in a small voice.

Ham looked so upset, Gretchen wanted to pat him on the head the way one might pat a dog. "Ham, let's just think about this for a minute. Can't we do a story on the cafeteria anyway? Why not write about something we know about. Like the way the food tastes. That's what the kids are interested in anyway.

They just want their hamburgers to taste better."

Ham looked a little less forlorn. "You mean we should write a story about what the kids like and don't like?"

"That would be a start, don't you think?"

Ham's expression turned admiring. "You're going to save the paper, Gretchen."

"Oh, Ham, don't be so dramatic." But she was pleased anyway.

By the time Gretchen got home, she was full of ideas about how they could write their cafeteria story. She could write about the kind of foods kids like and maybe include some ideas about good nutrition. She'd even include Mrs. Stewart's comments about how the cafeteria was run. Ham could do a survey to find out how students felt about the meals they were being served now. That, Gretchen thought with satisfaction, was solid journalism.

She was going to call Ham, but the phone rang. Well, it was probably him anyway, ready to discuss his own ideas.

But the voice on the other end of the line, though male, didn't belong to Ham. It was Tim.

"Hi, Gretchen, how are you doing?" he asked cheerfully.

Still flying high from her reporting breakthrough, Gretchen didn't feel quite so ill at ease as she might have. She felt pretty good in fact.

"I'm doing just fine."

"Well, I hope you're feeling as good on Saturday night, so we can go out together."

Tim was asking her out again. He must actually like her! Her next thought was that she should say no. She knew that was what she should say, but flashing before her eyes was the impression she had made on the girls by going out with Tim. If they knew that he had had such a good time that he wanted another date, if they actually saw her at the movies, holding hands with Tim . . . Gretchen could feel herself getting excited, and it wasn't because she had some ideas for a newspaper story.

"Gretchen, are you there?"

"Yes, I'm here."

"So how about it?"

Tell him no, an inner voice counseled. What else could she say? But then she had a thought. Mrs. Coppick was going to be here this weekend. There were probably all sorts of ways she could get out of the house without raising Mrs. Coppick's suspicions. Tim was waiting; she had to say something. So she said, "Yes."

"Great. Maybe we'll go to the movies."

Gretchen didn't care what they did. She was already standing in the middle of a circle of girls, telling them about her date for Saturday night. "Fine. Tim, call me Saturday morning to make arrangements." Her dad would be gone by then.

"Sure. Talk to you then."

Her high lasted most of the evening. When she crawled into bed, though, a few niggling thoughts were buzzing around. How was she going to get out of the house exactly? Would Robin help her? But Robin disapproved of her getting involved with Tim. Gretchen could feel her eyes growing heavier. She'd figure it all out later. In a few moments she was sound asleep.

C H A P T E R
ELEVEN

Gretchen found Robin on the school playground the next morning and quickly filled her in on Tim's call. She watched as the expression on Robin's face went from amazement to worry. "You actually said you were going?"

"I want to. And I think I can, if you help me."

"Oh, Gretchen," Robin groaned. "I don't think I should."

"How many times in my life am I going to date a real movie star?" Gretchen demanded. "I've got it all figured out. I tell Mrs. Coppick I'm going to your house for the evening. I meet Tim. We go to the movie and that's that."

"Your baby-sitter will let you go?"

"She's not exactly a baby-sitter," Gretchen

said huffily. "I'm a baby-sitter. Mrs. Coppick is just staying with me."

"Right, right," Robin said, dismissing the distinction. "But what if she won't let you?"

"I'll clear it with my dad before he goes."

The first bell started to ring, and the girls began walking toward the school. "I thought you were doing this to just win your bet with Veronica," Robin said.

"That's how it started, but this is so neat, Robin. He really likes me. Wouldn't you go if you had the chance?"

Robin looked troubled. "I'm not sure."

"This is the most exciting thing that has ever happened to me," Gretchen insisted.

"Oh, all right." Robin looked at her friend, hard. "If this is what you really want."

"It'll be great," Gretchen said happily. "I can hardly wait until I tell Veronica."

Her opportunity came at lunch. The girls were all sitting together, talking about who was going to summer camp. As casually as she could, Gretchen said, "I'm going somewhere this Saturday."

Her comment was drowned out in the conversation. "At my camp, there's riding every day," Veronica said.

"I'm going to computer camp," Kim informed them.

"I'm going out with Tim on Saturday," Gretchen said loudly.

It was worth all the risk she was going to have to go through just to see the girls' expressions, Gretchen thought with satisfaction. Four amazed faces were turned in her direction.

"He called you?" Sharon asked.

Gretchen laughed gaily. "Well, of course. How else could he ask me out?"

"Where are you going?" Kim demanded.

"To a movie, I guess."

"He still doesn't know how old you are, does he?" Natalie asked.

"No. But he's only three years older than me. That's not so much."

"Well, it might be," Veronica cut in smoothly. "This guy's an actor. He's sophisticated, Gretchen."

Just the kind of boy you think would be interested in you, Gretchen thought, noting how Veronica was clenching her hands in front of her. "Yeah. Isn't it terrific?"

After that the floodgates opened: what she should wear, how she should act, which way she should steer the conversation. It was as if she were the sun and all the planets were revolving around her. And it felt great.

The feeling of excitement only grew as the countdown to Saturday began. Oh, she tried to keep her mind on other things, especially helping Ham write an article about the cafeteria that wouldn't get them expelled. She also tried to get her father ready to go on his trip to Santa Fe.

On Thursday night, she sat on her father's bed, watching him search anxiously through his wardrobe, just the way she had been doing the past few days.

"I think you should take your blue sweater," she suggested.

"Do you? Maybe it'll be too hot for it."

"It might get cool at night."

Her father grabbed the sweater off its hanger. "Yeah, that's a good idea."

"Besides," Gretchen teased, "it matches your eyes."

"You're cute, kiddo." He flung the sweater on the bed.

"What time is Mrs. Coppick coming?"

"Saturday morning. She'll get here right before I leave."

"Dad," Gretchen began, "can I go over to Robin's on Saturday night?" Quickly she added, "Not a sleep-over. I'll be home by eleven."

"I guess that would be all right," Mr. Hubbard said absently as he examined his shirts. "But you'd better make it ten."

"Ten!" How could she ever explain to Tim that she had to be home at such an early hour?

"Ten's your curfew, Gretchen." He looked up. "Is there anything special going on that would make you want to change it?"

"Uh . . . no." She couldn't come up quickly enough with a lie that her dad would believe.

"All right, I'll tell Mrs. Coppick that you can go to Robin's for the evening and you'll be home by ten."

Gretchen knew she should have been elated, but all she felt was bad. Bad through and through. If her father found out that she was lying, he would be so upset with her. Mad, yes, but mostly disappointed. "I'm going to watch some television," she said, getting up.

Her father looked surprised. "Don't you want to help me some more? I was kind of enjoying your advice."

There was nothing Gretchen would have liked better. She had felt so close to her father as he tried to pick out the clothes that her mom might like. But now all she wanted to do was get out of the room and drown herself in some stupid TV show.

One thing Gretchen learned by Saturday was that no matter how you felt about a day coming, whether you wanted it to hurry or delay, it always got there in its own time. At various points during the week, she had felt both ways about Saturday. Now it was here.

She awoke to the doorbell's ringing. It was early. But her father had told her last night his cab was coming at seven. What a day not to be able to stay in bed. For once, she needed her beauty sleep.

Gretchen threw on her robe and headed downstairs. There in the middle of the kitchen stood her father with his suitcase and Mrs. Coppick, looking the way she always did— cheerful. In Gretchen's opinion, it was a bit early in the morning for the sunny smile that broke out as soon as Mrs. Coppick turned and saw Gretchen.

"Well, if it isn't my little bunny." Her chubby face practically quivered with excitement.

Gretchen shuddered. She had forgotten that particular endearment.

"Come over here and give me a big hug."

Gretchen cast a beseeching glance at her father, who could only offer a slight shrug in return.

"I haven't brushed my teeth," Gretchen

muttered, but she let herself be wrapped in Mrs. Coppick's voluminous arms anyway, her face crushed against the scratchy rayon of the woman's summer dress.

Mrs. Coppick held her at arm's length. "Why, you've lost so much weight." She turned anxiously to Mr. Hubbard. "She's not ill, is she?"

"I believe the weight loss was intended," her father said dryly.

"Well, I don't go with this notion of girls being too thin," Mrs. Coppick fretted.

Obviously, Gretchen thought, taking in her ample body. In that brown dress with the black dots on it, she looked like a plum pudding.

"This country is obsessed with weight," Mrs. Coppick continued. "It's unhealthy to be skinny. How do you keep your strength up if you don't eat?" She apparently didn't expect an answer to the question because she plowed on. "I'm going to make sure this little girl has plenty to eat while you're gone, Mr. Hubbard."

The taxi horn blared from the driveway. "I'm sure you two will work it out," Mr. Hubbard said hurriedly. "Come here and give me a kiss, kiddo."

Gretchen flew into his arms. "Have fun,"

she whispered. Even to her own ears, it sounded like a plea.

Her father held her close for a second then kissed her on the cheek.

"Oh, Dad, don't forget about tonight."

The taxi honked again.

"Right. Gretchen can go over to Robin's tonight. Home by ten." He quickly picked up his bag and opened the back door. "See you guys Monday night." Then he was gone.

As soon as he was out the door, Mrs. Coppick said, "How about some breakfast. You remember my waffles, don't you?" she asked tantalizingly.

Gretchen could see that if she wasn't careful, she'd put on ten pounds by this evening. Still, Mrs. Coppick did make awfully good waffles.

"Let me see if you have any real maple syrup," Mrs. Coppick said, opening one of the cabinets.

That was enough to spring Gretchen out of her reverie. "No," she said a little too loudly. "I mean, no thanks. Just an egg and toast."

Mrs. Coppick looked disappointed. Perhaps it was she who wanted the waffles. "Well, if you're sure."

"I am. I think I'll take a quick shower and get dressed." She wanted to be ready to answer the phone in case Tim called. But despite all her good planning, Gretchen was out in the yard, picking some tulips for Mrs. Coppick, when the phone rang.

She could hear it from the yard. She rushed inside as fast as she could, but Mrs. Coppick was already holding the receiver. "It's for you. A boy," she added disapprovingly.

Gretchen took the phone. How was she going to conduct date arrangements with Mrs. Coppick hovering over her?

"Gretchen, it's me, Ham."

"Ham!"

"You sound awfully happy to hear from me," Ham said suspiciously.

"Well, we've got to get that article for the school paper done."

Mrs. Coppick turned away and sat down at the kitchen table to read the newspaper.

Ham was puzzled. "I know that. Why do you think I'm calling? I finished the polling yesterday, and I wanted to see your rough draft of the 'Foods We'd Like to Eat' article. We're already late on this story. It absolutely has to be in on Monday."

She hadn't gotten around to writing it yet, but she didn't want to confess that to Ham. "Sure. How about tomorrow?"

"I can't tomorrow. We're driving up to Lake Vincent. What about this afternoon?"

Gretchen didn't want to do anything this afternoon but paint her nails and think about Tim. On the other hand, working with Ham would distract her—she glanced over at Mrs. Coppick—and get her out of the house.

"Okay. At the library?"

"It's really warm out. I don't want to be stuck in the library. Let's meet at the park."

"I'm going out to study later," Gretchen said after she hung up the phone.

"Oh." Mrs. Coppick positively drooped. "I thought we'd play a game of Monopoly."

Well, at least Mrs. Coppick had gotten past Candy Land. "Maybe tomorrow," Gretchen said to appease her. Who knew? Tomorrow a game of Monopoly might sound awfully good.

She spent the rest of the morning working on her story and, once again, looking through her closet. Finally she decided on the sleeveless dress she had bought in Santa Fe. It was cute without being dressy, and Gretchen had to admit it showed off her figure. The whole time she kept waiting for the phone to ring. When it finally did, she yelled downstairs, "I've got it." Breathlessly she picked up the phone and said, "Hello."

"You sound like you've been running."
Tim's warm voice came over the wire.

"Just hurrying to get the phone," Gretchen
replied.

"Well, I'm glad you're so anxious to hear
from me." Tim chuckled.

Gretchen didn't know what to say. She
hadn't meant it like that.

"Are we still on for tonight?" Tim asked.

"Sure." She took a breath. "I thought
maybe I could meet you at the movies. There's
a sci-fi flick playing. It starts at seven."

"You must be reading my mind. I don't
drive yet, you know," Tim said, sounding embarrassed. "I can walk to the movies but I can
always bring you home in a cab. There are
usually some at the train station, aren't
there?"

"Sure." She wondered if she should mention her curfew now, but she thought better of
it. No need to have a silly curfew hanging over
their heads.

"All right. See you in front of the theater at
seven, then?"

"Seven." Gretchen unsteadily put the
phone down. She was actually going to be
doing this.

She looked at the clock and noticed it was
time to meet Ham. By the time she had ped-

aled over to the park, Ham was sitting on one of the benches, looking through a folder of papers. "Hi," he said, a big smile creasing his face as she parked her bike and sat down next to him.

"So how's it going?"

"Here are the results of my unscientific poll," he said, handing a messy paper over to her.

Gretchen's eyes widened as she read it. "Only twelve percent of the kids said they liked the food."

"Right. Wait till Stewball sees this. She'll have to do something about it."

"She won't be happy," Gretchen warned.

"And look at this," Ham said, turning the piece of paper over. "Seventy-one percent said they'd eat in the cafeteria instead of bringing their lunch if the food was better."

"More profit for the school district."

"This is even better than proving the mystery meat is dog food. This is about giving the people what they want!"

Gretchen couldn't help grinning at Ham. He looked so pleased with himself. "Here's a rough draft of my article," she said, handing it over. "I'll work on it tomorrow, and I promise it will fit right in with this survey."

"You know, Gretchen, I would have made a

big mess of this whole story if it hadn't been for you," Ham said shyly.

"Oh, you would have pulled it out."

He shook his head. "No way."

"Way," Gretchen said with a laugh.

"I think it's going to be good, don't you?" Ham sounded anxious.

"Yes, I do."

Looking up at a bird that had perched on a branch above them, Ham asked, "Did you know there's going to be a graduation dance?"

"Of course. Robin's writing an article about it."

"Yeah, right. Well, the thing is, some people are going with"—he choked a little on the word—"dates."

"Robin and Jon maybe, and some of the others, but not all the kids." Poor Ham must be worried about trying to find a girl to go with. In his case, it might be a problem.

"Want to go with me?" he blurted out.

Gretchen looked at him, stunned. Ham asking her out was the last thing on her mind. What would Veronica say if Gretchen actually showed up at the dance with Ham? Going from Tim to Ham was like going from the sublime to the ridiculous.

Ham licked his lips. "I guess you don't want to go."

"Oh, I didn't say that," Gretchen said, stalling for time.

"Then you do?" he asked hopefully.

I didn't say that either, she thought. "I guess I'm not sure." She was trying to be nice, but Ham looked so crestfallen that she felt terrible. "Probably I can."

Immediately perking up, Ham said, "Great! Just great! We'll have a great time."

"I said probably." Gretchen weakly backtracked.

"Sure. Just let me know." But he looked as though he thought the date was in the bag.

As she biked slowly home, Gretchen wondered how she had gotten into this situation. Last fall, she had been a fat kid whose only worry was where her next ice-cream cone was coming from. Now she had an actor to impress, on one hand, and the responsibility for Ham's good time at the graduation dance, on the other. It all seemed like a burden, and she didn't feel ready for any of it.

Her rotten mood held as she got ready for her date. Instead of being excited and happy, as she had thought she would be, she just felt sick, sometimes feverish, sometimes queasy. The last thing she felt like doing was eating, but when she came down to supper, she found that Mrs. Coppick had kept her promise of tempting Gretchen with some serious food. Two golden, crisp pork chops lay on a platter next to a bowl of fluffy mashed potatoes oozing butter. There was escalloped apples as a side dish. Gretchen hadn't eaten anything so heavy in months.

"Are you hungry?" Mrs. Coppick asked happily.

"Not too," Gretchen said, sitting down at the table.

"Oh, but you have to eat." She served her a pork chop and then put a heaping spoonful of potatoes on the plate. "Take some apples, too," Mrs. Coppick urged.

Dutifully Gretchen took some of the apples. You don't have to eat this, she told herself. You don't want this.

But a funny thing happened. After a few tentative bites, Gretchen found that she was ravenous. The food was delicious, and to her surprise, it seemed to quell the uncertain feelings in her stomach.

When she was finally finished, after a second helping of potatoes and apples, she once again felt terrible. What had she done? And right before her date, too. True, she had a long walk ahead of her, but she'd have to walk to California to get rid of the calories in this meal.

"I have to go," she said, throwing her napkin down at the table.

"I'll drive you," Mrs. Coppick said promptly.

"Oh, no." She gave a false little laugh. "I need my exercise after that meal. It was wonderful, though."

"Thank you," Mrs. Coppick said modestly. "It was good. Tomorrow I thought I'd make my Hungarian goulash."

Swell, Gretchen thought. "I'd better go now."

"See you at ten, then. You will be getting a ride home?"

"Yes." Mrs. Coppick would freak if she saw a taxi drive up. Maybe she could say the Millers' car broke down if she was caught.

Once she was out of the house, Gretchen checked her purse to make sure she had her makeup. To her horror, she saw a small grease spot on her dress. Why hadn't she waited to put it on until after she had eaten? There was nothing to do about it now. If she didn't leave, she'd be late. It'll be dark in the theater, she told herself.

The walk was long, as Gretchen knew it would be. She'd probably have stains under her armpits as well as a spot on her dress.

Whatever excitement she had felt about the date was dripping away. Now she just wanted this night to be over.

Finally, after stopping to put on her makeup, she approached the outskirts of downtown Forest Glen. The movie theater was right in the middle of the downtown. It was an old-fashioned place that had just one movie screen instead of five like the theater in the mall. As she got closer, she could see a line waiting to get in to the movie. She had forgotten the theater could be crowded on a Saturday night.

Tim was waiting right in front of the box office, as cute as ever. But then Gretchen noticed something else. Friends of her parents, Mr. and Mrs. Barnett, were talking to each other at the head of the line.

Gretchen panicked. Now what? Mr. Barnett owned the hardware store right across the street from her father's garage. There was no way he wouldn't mention that he had seen Gretchen at the movies with a boy.

Tim walked up to her. "Hi." He smiled. "How're you doing?"

Gretchen pulled him toward the corner. Fortunately Mr. and Mrs. Barnett were so deep in conversation they didn't notice her.

was practically deserted, except for one couple pushing their toddler in a baby swing.

"This *is* kind of neat," Tim said. "Shall we climb in?"

It wasn't that easy for Gretchen in her dress, but she followed Tim up the wooden ladder. The floor of the fort was dirty. Tim took off his jacket and spread it down for Gretchen to sit on. "Thanks," she said. Maybe this wasn't so bad after all.

"I like it here. Good view. Private."

"You should see it on Saturday mornings. It's crawling with kids."

"Well, on Saturday night, it's ours."

Before Gretchen knew what he was doing, Tim snaked his arm around her shoulder, leaned his face close, and kissed her. Well, tried anyway. As soon as she saw him coming toward her, she jerked her head violently to the side.

"Hey!" Tim said, surprised.

"What are you doing?" she cried.

"Well, I was trying to kiss you," Tim replied in a huffy tone.

"Why would you do that?"

"You were the one who wanted to skip the movie. I *thought*," he said sarcastically, "that's what you had in mind."

Gretchen could feel the tears forming behind her eyes. "No."

Now that it was obvious Gretchen was honestly upset, Tim looked more confused than angry. "I don't get it. You're acting like you've never been alone with a boy before."

"I haven't," she whispered. Then, before she could stop herself, she said, "I'm only twelve."

"What?"

The tears started falling down her cheeks.

"But you look like you go to high school." His tone turned accusing. "You said you went to high school."

"I never said that."

"You never said you didn't."

Gretchen reached for her purse and searched through her bag for a tissue.

Tim shook his head. "Twelve."

"I'm sorry. I should have told you. It was stupid, I know."

"It sure was. Or I was the stupid one," he added bitterly.

She thought about explaining, telling him about the bet, but that would probably make her seem even more like a twelve-year-old. "I think I'd better go home now."

"Do you want me to take you?" Tim asked unenthusiastically.

"No. It's not even eight o'clock. I can walk."

"Are you sure?"

"Yes."

"All right." He began climbing down the wooden ladder.

That's the last I'll see of him, she thought morosely. The tears started to flow harder.

A few moments later, Tim's head popped back into view. Gretchen's heart rose.

"I forgot my jacket."

"Your . . ."

"You're sitting on it."

Gretchen lifted herself and shook out the jacket to get rid of the dirt.

"Thanks," he said, grabbing it from her. Then he really was gone.

C H A P T E R

TWELVE

It had been a long walk to the movie theater. It seemed like an even longer walk home.

Gretchen was glad she knew how to take side streets and avoid the areas where her friends lived. She would have died if they saw her like this, crumpled, crying, her makeup a mess.

It occurred to her she might have trouble getting into the house without Mrs. Coppick seeing her, but she sneaked around to the garage door and let herself in through the back. Hearing the television blaring in the den, Gretchen knew she could make it to her room without being seen.

As soon as she got in her room, she tossed off

her dress and threw it in the closet. She didn't care if she never wore it again. After changing into her oldest, rattiest jeans and a sweatshirt, she went into the hall bathroom and scrubbed her face. Peering into the mirror, she saw she no longer looked as if she'd been crying, or wearing makeup, for that matter. She once again looked twelve.

There was no putting off the inevitable. If she stayed upstairs, Gretchen knew Mrs. Coppick would eventually hear her and assume there was a burglar in the house or something. She'd better get downstairs.

"Gretchen!" Mrs. Coppick said with a start, looking up from her television show. "When did you come in?"

"A little while ago."

"Why didn't you say hello? Why were you sneaking around?"

"I just went upstairs to change." She couldn't tell one more lie. Mrs. Coppick was right. She had been sneaking around.

Mrs. Coppick peered at her. "What's wrong, bunny?"

"Don't call me that, please."

"You girls. I forget how it is when you get older. I made a cake," she added brightly.

Cake. Well, actually, she was in the mood

for cake. Why shouldn't she eat cake like everyone else did? "Fine. Is there any ice cream to go with it?"

"I believe there is."

Gretchen went out to the kitchen and deliberately cut herself a huge piece. Then she scooped some vanilla ice cream on top. This ought to make her feel better.

She sat down at the kitchen table and started eating. Even though she was barely tasting the concoction, she kept swallowing methodically. When she was done, she couldn't say she had enjoyed it, but she did feel full.

Mrs. Coppick came into the kitchen. "Do you want to watch television with me? There's a wrestling match on soon. I do so like wrestling."

"Thanks, but I'm tired. I'm going to go to bed."

"I forgot to ask, did you have fun tonight?"

Gretchen tried to smile, but it came out as more of a grimace. "It was different."

Maybe it was because she wasn't used to eating so much in an evening, or maybe it was just the night's events, but Gretchen lay uncomfortably in bed for hours. Waiting for sleep gave her plenty of time to go over her date, if you could call it that, in detail. How could she have not known the whole thing would blow up in her face? And what was she going to tell her friends? She asked herself that several times over the course of the evening. She had longed so much to change her life. She had, but things were nothing the way she thought they would be.

As she finally drifted off to sleep, she remembered how remarkable it had seemed that reality could be better than fantasy. What a joke. Disasters like this were the kind of thing that happened in real life. From now on she'd just live her life in her head, the way she used to.

The next day, the phone started ringing almost immediately. Sharon called first, and Gretchen told her a story as close to the truth as possible: She had seen her parents' friends at the theater, and so she suggested to Tim that they sit in the park for a while. Then she went home.

"That's it?" Sharon asked, disappointed. "Did he say he wants to see you again?"

"I think he figured out I wasn't in high school yet."

"Oh, well," Sharon said loyally. "You still had a date with an actor. That's something."

But Gretchen didn't feel like it was such a big deal. She got more and more depressed as

next she answered questions from Natalie—
the first time *she* had ever phoned—and finally from Robin.

Robin immediately knew that something
was wrong. "You're not telling me the whole
story, are you?"

"No," Gretchen whispered. To Robin, she
spilled out the rest of it.

"Oh, Gretchen." Robin sighed. "I'm sorry."

"I should have known he was way out of my
league."

"He was just too old for you."

"Things were a lot easier when I was fat."

"No, they weren't. You were miserable."

"Well, I'm not exactly happy now."

After she hung up, Gretchen's mood deep-
ened. She spent the rest of the afternoon pol-
ishing her article, playing Monopoly, and eating the rest of Mrs. Coppick's cake.

By the time she woke up for school the next
morning, she was afraid to get on the scale.
She felt enormous, and when it came time to
get dressed, she put on an old pair of slacks
with an elastic waist and a sloppy T-shirt. She
didn't bother putting gel on her hair.

When Gretchen arrived at school, Robin did
a double take, but she didn't say anything.
Veronica, however, did.

"What happened to you?" Veronica demanded as the girls came up to her.

"Nothing."

"Well, how was your date?"

"Fine."

"Natalie told me you didn't go to the movies."

"I'm sure Natalie told you the whole story," Gretchen said, trying to move past Veronica.

"Did he kiss you?" Veronica asked.

Gretchen didn't know what to say to that. Finally she just shook her head and walked into school. A few kids gave her an odd look, and Gretchen waited to see if they would treat her differently. No one did, at least, not that she could tell. Even Ham, who was probably regretting his invitation to the dance, just started talking to her about her article.

"Did you finish it?" he asked.

She pulled it out of her notebook. "Right here."

Ham stood in front of her and read it. "It's great! Just what I had in mind." He looked up at Gretchen. "Hey, what's wrong?"

"What do you mean?" she said, bristling.

"Well, usually you're so excited about stuff. You look like your best friend died. But, hey," he joked, "there's Robin right over there."

"Ha, ha."

Ham looked crestfallen. "I was only trying to be funny."

Gretchen stomped over to her desk. She shouldn't take her feelings out on Ham, she knew, but she couldn't help it. Everything seemed as black as dirt this morning.

Gretchen was dreading lunch. Now would be the time when the girls would have at her, asking their millions of questions. Defiantly, she bought the macaroni and cheese and a cookie. If she was going to have to face a table-ful of sixth-grade inquisitors, she was going to do it on a full stomach.

Her tray did cause a few raised eyebrows. Before anyone could ask, she crisply told her now-familiar story to the girls who hadn't heard it, ending with the face-saving comment "It was neat, but let's face it, he is a little old for me."

Most of the girls seemed to believe her. Only Veronica gave her a long appraising glance. Kim started talking about the graduation dance, which, to Gretchen's relief, got the girls off the topic of her and Tim. She supposed she could mention that Ham wanted to take her, but she knew that news would thrust her unwelcomely into the spotlight once more.

When the day finally ended, Gretchen gathered up her books and stuffed them into her bag. Robin appeared at her side. "Want to come over after school?"

Gretchen just wanted to get home. "I can't," she said. "I'd better get home."

"Your dad's coming back tonight, isn't he?"

With everything else that had been happening, Gretchen hadn't had much time to think about that. If her dad returned with the news her mother wasn't coming back, Gretchen didn't know how she would stand it. It would be the last straw.

"Have you heard from Dad?" Gretchen asked Mrs. Coppick as soon as she walked in the door.

Mrs. Coppick shook her head. "He said he'd be home around dinnertime. I made a pot roast and left it in the oven for you. All you have to do is heat it up."

Gretchen knew she should go upstairs to do her homework, but she went into the den, turned on the television, and watched mindlessly for an hour or so. The chime clock on the mantel was striking five-thirty when her father walked through the door.

Squeezing her eyes tight, she whispered a little prayer. Then she ran into the living room to greet him. The moment she saw him, she knew. He was talking to Mrs. Coppick about his bumpy airplane ride, but his eyes were all lit up, and he was gesturing animatedly with his hands.

Gretchen threw herself into his arms. "Mom's coming home, isn't she?"

"She is," he said, kissing her all over her forehead and hair. "I'll tell you all about it later."

It seemed to take forever for Mrs. Coppick to get paid, show Mr. Hubbard the roast, and tell him how much she enjoyed staying with Gretchen again.

When the door finally closed behind Mrs. Coppick, Gretchen pulled her father over to the kitchen table and said, "Now tell me everything."

Her father laughed. "Your mother made me promise to wait until she called this evening, so we could both tell you the whole story, but that's one promise I'm not going to be able to keep, I see."

"No way."

"It was a very nice trip. It was a little awkward at first. After all, I hadn't seen your mother since Christmas, but we did some sight-seeing and we talked . . . a lot. Now that your mother has a year of teaching under her belt, she thinks she may be able to find a job here. If she can't she'll spend her time doing her own writing."

"I knew she missed us too much to stay away."

"She finally decided that. I think it had a lot to do with your visit." Mr. Hubbard smiled.

"And with yours."

"You're right."

Later that night, her mother told her the same thing. "After I saw you both, I just didn't want to stay away anymore. The other stuff will work itself out. But I don't think I would have known that if I hadn't been away. The only thing I regret is how hard it's been on you."

Gretchen cradled the phone close to her ear. "I missed you so much," she said in a low voice.

"Well, I'll be home in a few weeks. But, darling, this year has been good for you, too. You lost all that weight. You've really grown up. I'm so proud of you, Gretchen."

Gretchen wondered how proud her mother would be if she knew what had been going on the last couple of weeks.

"Why, you're like a different person," her mother continued.

"Sometimes I feel like I don't know who I am," Gretchen said.

"You're a mix of the old and the new. Just because you've matured and lost some weight doesn't mean you're not the same wonderful girl you've always been," her mother replied, surprised.

Gretchen thought about that comment as she got ready for bed. Was she the same wonderful person? Had she been wonderful before? She didn't feel too good about herself now. Was that what being thin and grown-up meant? Having plenty of opportunities to do things you probably shouldn't? Gretchen had a strange longing, like a hunger, to put everything back the way it was.

If that's really what she wanted, stepping on the scale the next morning showed her she was on the road to return. She had gained two pounds.

First, she panicked. Then she went downstairs and had a doughnut and milk for breakfast. Idly she wondered what would happen if she actually put back all her weight. It felt kind of nice. Safe, anyway.

The next few days passed in a kind of limbo. Gretchen ate what she wanted, though never as much as she had packed in over the weekend. She gained back another pound. She didn't peruse her closet for just the right outfit either, instead choosing whatever she had that was clean. A haircut was in order, too, but she didn't bother to make an appointment. Things went on like that for most of the week. On Friday, though, she decided that she ought to make some effort to get dressed up. The newspaper was coming out that morning, and it seemed like she owed it to Ham and the rest of the staff to at least look presentable.

Ham was wearing out the floor of Mrs. Volini's room when Gretchen arrived. The printer was supposed to have delivered the paper a half hour earlier. "They're not here!"

"They'll get here."

"Do you think so?" Ham looked at her with pleading eyes.

"Yes, of course. The delivery truck could have gotten stuck in traffic or . . ."

Before Gretchen could come up with another reason, Mrs. Volini came in the room, carrying a bundle of news sheets. "They've arrived," she said gaily.

"Let's see one," Ham yelped.

Mrs. Volini snipped the string and handed copies of the *Voice* to Ham and Gretchen. Then she opened one herself.

Gretchen and Ham pored over the front page. The headline read "Cafeteria Food

Needs an Upgrade." Below was a picture of the garbage can in the cafeteria stuffed with half-eaten lunches.

"Powerful stuff," Gretchen whispered. Then she nudged Ham. Mrs. Volini was frowning.

"Did I see this picture before it went in the paper?" the teacher demanded.

"We were going to have the picture of the kids eating in the lunchroom, but that one didn't come out very well," Ham said in a small voice. "So we substituted."

"And you didn't clear it?"

"You were absent that day. Remember?"

Mrs. Volini shook her head. "You know, I let this article about the cafeteria run because you seemed to have all your facts right and it was an issue of interest to your readers. But frankly, Ham, I think this photograph is sensational. And I don't mean in a good kind of way," she added sternly.

Gretchen was all ready to apologize, but Ham, to her amazement, went on the offensive. "I'm sorry I didn't check with you, Mrs. Volini, but I think this picture is good journalism."

"Oh, you do."

"Yes, I do. This picture shows just what the

kids think of their lunches better than any poll could."

A smile twitched around Mrs. Volini's lips. "You know, Kevin, when you decided to investigate this story, I told you you would have to put up with whatever flak came from running it. Are you still prepared for that?"

Ham nodded. "I think it's a great story. We'll be in junior high next year, but maybe the other kids will get a decent meal."

"That's what journalism can do, make things happen." She put out her hand for Ham to shake. "I think you've made a fine editor."

The room was filling up with students, eagerly grabbing papers. "Good thing we didn't go with the dog-food story." Gretchen laughed.

"Yeah, she probably would have hit me with that hand," Ham agreed.

The newspaper was a gigantic success. Everyone was talking about the cafeteria story, but there were some other surprising successes as well.

Veronica's "Safe at Second," as she called her sports column, was actually funny. She wrote about how a baseball game appeared to someone who had no idea what was going on.

The other big hit was Jonathan and Jason's

gossip column. In it, they pretended that they were at a pajama party, dished all kinds of gossip, and paired up couples, mostly from the sixth grade. Everyone wanted to be mentioned in it, but Gretchen scanned the column with trepidation. Bobby knew all about her and Tim, of course, though she wondered if he had heard the awful end to the story. He hadn't said a word, if he did know.

Finally she found her name near the bottom. "What about Gretchen?" the column read. "Is she going to give up movie stars for newspaper editors?"

She put down the paper with a sigh of relief. That wasn't too bad. It sounded as if she were the one who would be deciding whether or not to still see Tim. As for newspaper editors, well, that meant that Ham must have been talking. Still, it could have been worse.

In honor of the newspaper, Mrs. Volini had planned a party for last period—not that much got done the rest of the day. At lunchtime, Ham was invited to a meeting with the principal and Mrs. Stewart about the article on the cafeteria, so right before the party began he stood up to give his report.

"Well, it didn't go too bad," he began. "Mrs. Stewart sat there looking like she was going to take a bite out of me instead of one of her Wednesday specials. . . ."

"Kevin . . . ," Mrs. Volini said warningly.

"But she didn't. Actually, at the end of the meeting, she looked kind of sad and said she didn't realize the kids hated the cafeteria food so much. Mr. Thomas said he had heard they served really good lunches over at Kimball Junior High, so he and Mrs. Stewart are going over there to sample the food."

The class cheered. Then the party began in earnest.

Gretchen was feeling pretty good about herself. She was taking compliments from the kids about the newspaper, when Veronica came up. Feeling charitable, Gretchen said, "That was a cool column, Veronica."

"Thank you," Veronica said. "But speaking of cool, what's happened to you lately, Gretchen?"

Gretchen flushed. She didn't want to talk about this, especially here.

Veronica pulled her off to a corner. "Now don't think I'm just being mean to you."

"Aren't you?"

"Not exactly." She scowled. "Anyway, I'm just telling you this for your own good."

"I don't suppose I'll be able to stop you," Gretchen said bitterly.

"No." Veronica sat on top of a desk. "Now the way I see it, you kind of freaked out after your date with Tim. You couldn't handle being cool, right?"

Gretchen didn't say anything, so Veronica just continued.

"I don't know what really happened between you and Tim, but hey, he asked you out, so you couldn't have been that weird. And let's face it, he was too old for you. But just because it didn't work out doesn't mean you have to go back to being a fat nerd," Veronica said bluntly. "What's the point of that?"

"Well, thank you for your advice," Gretchen said.

Veronica thought she was serious. She slid off the desk and said, "You're welcome."

Mrs. Volini was cutting pieces from a huge cake the shape of a newspaper with "the Voice" written in black icing. Gretchen didn't feel like having any. However, Ham walked over to her and handed her a slice on a paper plate.

"For you."

"I'm not sure if I'm eating cake these days or not," she said, putting it down on her desk.

Ham was concentrating on eating his own piece of cake. "Boy, I wish we hadn't started this newspaper so late in the year. I really would have liked to put out another edition."

"There's a monthly paper at the junior high."

Ham looked up. "I'm going to sign up to work on it."

"Me, too." For the first time she felt some stirring of excitement about junior high.

"Hey, Gretchen. Have you thought about going to the dance with me?"

Gretchen decided she could ask Ham a question. "You never would have invited me if I were fat, would you?"

Ham answered her honestly. "Probably not."

"So being thin makes all the difference."

"I'm not that thin," Ham said. "But that's not why people didn't pay attention to you then. In spite of all that tonnage you were carrying around, it was like you weren't even here. You never said anything."

Had losing weight made her eager to start participating more, or had the need to break out of her shell finally put her on a diet? Gretchen wasn't sure.

"Are you going to eat that cake or just stare at it?" Ham asked. "You don't have to eat the whole thing. You can just have a little."

She spooned off a large bite. "Pretty good."
Then she put the rest back on the desk.

"So what about the dance?" Ham asked.
"You never answered me."

"Didn't I?" Gretchen replied. "I'll go."